FOUR H[illegible] GUNS. . .

Clint didn't move a muscle. He was facing four men with rifles, and he had no idea how proficient they were.

"Well," he said to McGirt, "if you're going to earn your money, let's get to it."

"In good time."

"You sure you don't want to try me alone?" Clint asked. "Be a feather in your cap if you took me yourself, you know."

McGirt just smiled. Then there was a shot!

At the sound of the shot, the Gunsmith drew his gun. McGirt's attention was diverted by the sound, and by the time he recovered it was too late. As he tried to bring his rifle to bear on Clint, Clint fired. The bullet struck McGirt in the chest, knocking him backward.

Clint dropped into a crouch just as another gunman fired. The bullet went over his head and struck the mirror behind the bar. He fired, and the other man went staggering out through the door.

Clint rolled this time, across the floor as the other two men fired . . .

* * *

Also in THE GUNSMITH series

MACKLIN'S WOMEN
THE CHINESE GUNMAN
BULLETS AND BALLOTS
THE RIVERBOAT GANG
KILLER GRIZZLY
NORTH OF THE BORDER
EAGLE'S GAP
CHINATOWN HELL
THE PANHANDLE SEARCH
WILDCAT ROUNDUP
THE PONDEROSA WAR
TROUBLE RIDES A FAST HORSE
DYNAMITE JUSTICE
THE POSSE
NIGHT OF THE GILA
THE BOUNTY WOMEN
WILD BILL'S GHOST
THE MINER'S SHOWDOWN
ARCHER'S REVENGE
SHOWDOWN IN RATON
WHEN LEGENDS MEET
DESERT HELL
THE DIAMOND GUN
DENVER DUO
HELL ON WHEELS
THE LEGEND MAKER
WALKING DEAD MAN
CROSSFIRE MOUNTAIN
THE DEADLY HEALER
THE TRAIL DRIVE WAR
GERONIMO'S TRAIL
THE COMSTOCK GOLD FRAUD
TEXAS TRACKDOWN
THE FAST DRAW LEAGUE
SHOWDOWN IN RIO MALO
OUTLAW TRAIL
HOMESTEADER GUNS
FIVE CARD DEATH
TRAILDRIVE TO MONTANA
TRIAL BY FIRE
THE OLD WHISTLER GANG
THE NEVADA TIMBER WAR
NEW MEXICO SHOWDOWN
BARBED WIRE AND BULLETS
DEATH EXPRESS
WHEN LEGENDS DIE
SIX-GUN JUSTICE
MUSTANG HUNTERS
TEXAS RANSOM
VENGEANCE TOWN
WINNER TAKE ALL
MESSAGE FROM A DEAD MAN
RIDE FOR VENGEANCE
THE TAKERSVILLE SHOOT
BLOOD ON THE LAND
SIX-GUN SIDESHOW
MISSISSIPPI MASSACRE
THE ARIZONA TRIANGLE
BROTHERS OF THE GUN
THE STAGECOACH THIEVES
JUDGMENT AT FIRECREEK
DEAD MAN'S JURY
HANDS OF THE STRANGLER
NEVADA DEATH TRAP
WAGON TRAIN TO HELL
RIDE FOR REVENGE
DEAD RINGER
TRAIL OF THE ASSASSIN
SHOOT-OUT AT CROSSFORK
BUCKSKIN'S TRAIL
HELLDORADO
THE HANGING JUDGE
THE BOUNTY HUNTER
TOMBSTONE AT LITTLE HORN
KILLER'S RACE
WYOMING RANGE WAR
GRAND CANYON GOLD
GUNS DON'T ARGUE
GUNDOWN
FRONTIER JUSTICE
GAME OF DEATH
THE OREGON STRANGLER
BLOOD BROTHERS
SCARLET FURY
ARIZONA AMBUSH
THE VENGEANCE TRAIL
THE DEADLY DERRINGER
THE STAGECOACH KILLERS
FIVE AGAINST DEATH
MUSTANG MAN

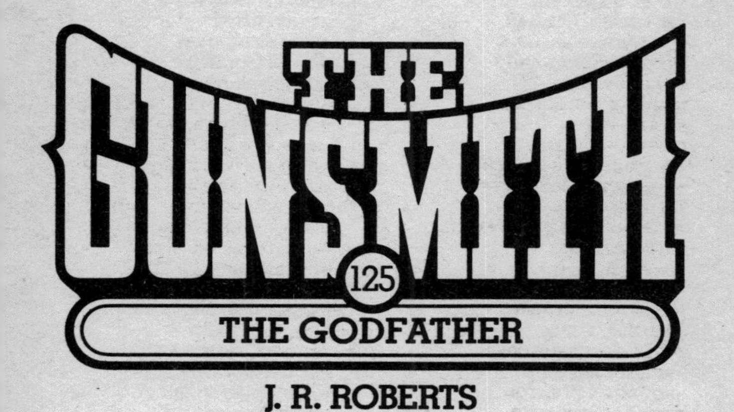

J. R. ROBERTS

JOVE BOOKS, NEW YORK

THE GODFATHER

A Jove Book / published by arrangement with
the author

PRINTING HISTORY
Jove edition / May 1992

ISBN: 0-515-10851-0

Jove Books are published by The Berkley Publishing Group,
200 Madison Avenue, New York, New York 10016.
The name "JOVE" and the "J" logo
are trademarks belonging to Jove Publications, Inc.

PRINTED IN THE UNITED STATES OF AMERICA

10 9 8 7 6 5 4 3 2 1

THE
GUNSMITH
125
THE GODFATHER

ONE

It was funny that he should find a baby, just a couple of days after he'd been talking about babies with Gena Miles. . . .

Clint met Gena in the town of Sutter, Kansas. He was passing through on his way to Texas, and had dinner in a small café a couple of blocks from his hotel. The café was run by Gena and her husband, Henry.

As soon as he met Gena, Clint wondered how she had ended up marrying the likes of Henry Miles. In front of all of their customers Miles had shouted at her, calling her slow and stupid. Gena had ducked her head, and in trying to serve faster, had dropped a tray of food. Again, Henry Miles had berated her in front of the diners. Miles, who appeared to be in his fifties, a good twenty-five years older than his wife, treated her more like an employee than a wife.

To Clint, Gena Miles looked as fragile as a string of pearls, and she had the same complexion. She was pale and pretty, with long brown hair that was damp at the ends from working in the café all day. Her form was slender but attractive, and she certainly did not seem like the kind of woman who would be married to a large, heavy man like Henry Miles.

"Why do you let him treat you that way?" he asked her when she brought him more coffee.

Her eyes widened in surprise at the question.

"He's my husband." She said it as if that explained it away.

"That doesn't give him the right to mistreat you," he said.

She didn't seem to understand the statement, and Clint felt sorry for her. As she started away, he wrapped his hand around her slender wrist.

"A woman as pretty as you are shouldn't be mistreated by her husband," he said softly. "You should be cherished and loved."

"Oh, my . . ." she said before she was able to stop herself. She touched her face and asked, "Do you really think I'm pretty?"

"Of course," he said. "Hasn't he ever told you that?"

"No," she said. "Henry is not much for compliments."

A thoughtful look on her face, she went about her business of serving the other tables, but every so often she would look over at Clint, who would smile at her.

That night Clint went back to his hotel and thought about Gena Miles—although at that point he didn't yet know her name. He decided to stay in town at least another day, and to have breakfast at the café in the morning.

He went to breakfast the following morning, thinking that maybe the man had been in a bad mood the night before. Maybe he didn't always treat his wife that way.

Over breakfast, he saw that he was wrong.

Breakfast was a busy time, and once again Henry Miles berated his wife in front of customers for serving too slowly.

"I don't know why she puts up with it," a woman at a nearby table said to her husband. Clint looked at the couple, who both appeared to be in their fifties.

"Now Martha—" her husband said.

"I mean it," feisty Martha said. "If you treated me like that I'd hit you with a frying pan."

The man smiled and put his hand over his wife's.

"I know you would, Martha."

"Henry Miles treated his first wife the same way, and he worked her to death before she was forty. I hope he doesn't do the same thing to Gena. I should have a talk with her."

"Now, Martha," her husband said, his tone turning stern, "we shouldn't get involved."

"Nonsense," she said. "Henry Miles has been a bully ever since we were all children. Gena never should have married him. She should have waited for a man her own age. Now that she is married to him, though, she shouldn't let him mistreat her so."

"We all know why they married," her husband said. "It was convenient for both of them. She needed a husband, and he needed help here in the café—help that he didn't have to pay."

"She should have babies," the woman said, "and Henry Miles will never give her any. He hates children. Poor Nancy was my friend, and she died barren and old before her time because of that man. I hate him."

"Shhh, Martha," the husband said. "There's nothing we can do."

"Well, somebody should do something."

"Quiet, here she comes," her husband warned. "Don't say anything."

You can learn a lot just from listening to other people's conversations. Clint had found that out a long time ago. He knew all he needed to know, now, about Henry and Gena Miles, and agreed with the older woman: Somebody should do something.

Gena had greeted him cheerfully, with a smile, remembering him from the night before. Now he called her over and asked for more coffee. Her husband may have been mean and a fool, but he was a good cook, and he made good coffee.

When she brought him the coffee he pointed to the table the older couple had just vacated.

"Who were those people?" he asked her.

"Oh, that was John and Martha. The last name is Novack. They own the general store. Why?"

"Oh," he said, "I overheard some of their conversation. She sounds like a very intelligent woman."

"Martha's a dear," Gena said. She started to turn away, but her curiosity got the better of her. "What were they talking about?"

He looked up into her wide, clear blue eyes and said, "They were talking about you."

"Me?" she said. She had the coffeepot in one hand and pressed her other hand to her breast. "What were they saying?"

"Gena," her husband shouted from the kitchen, "get your lazy ass in here!"

"Meet me later, and I'll tell you," Clint said to her.

"I can't," she said, looking alarmed. "I'm married."

"Yes," he said, "to a fool."

She dropped her hand to her side and he took her by the wrist, as he had last night.

"Gena!"

"I won't let go until you agree to meet me."

She looked around, unsure about what to do.

"Damn it, Gena!"

"All right!" she said to Clint.

"Where? When?"

She told him that she would be able to get away after the lunch rush but that she had to be back for dinner. She instructed him to ride south of town until he came to a big, twisted tree by a stream, and she would meet him there at two o'clock.

"All right," he said, releasing her wrist. "Until two."

She rushed toward the kitchen but threw him a glance over her shoulder before entering.

"Gen-a!"

"I'm coming. . . ."

As Clint left the café that morning it never occurred to him that he should be minding his own business.

TWO

Clint had no problem finding the twisted tree by the stream. He dismounted, not bothering to tie Duke's reins. The big black gelding wouldn't be going anywhere.

The spot was pretty and cool, and he didn't mind waiting, but right around two-thirty he decided that if Gena didn't show up, he'd just forget about her and leave town the next morning.

He was about to give up when he heard a horse approaching at a fast pace, and then he saw her. He watched as she approached, admiring the way she rode.

When she reached him she dismounted and started to apologize.

"I'm sorry I'm late, but Henry had me—"

"Hey, hey," he said, interrupting her, "you don't have to apologize to me."

"I don't?"

"No," he said. "In fact, you didn't even have to come if you didn't want to."

"And you wouldn't have been angry?"

"No."

She stared at him, shaking her head.

"You're certainly not anything like my husband."

"That's what I wanted to talk to you about."

"My husband?"

"Why'd you marry him?"

"I thought we were gonna talk about what John and Martha were saying about me."

"We are."

She stared at him and said, "You mean they were talking about my marriage."

"That's right," he said. "I got the impression that it wasn't a very happy one."

She turned her back on him and walked toward the stream. She was wearing jeans and a man's shirt, and although the shirt was big on her, the jeans weren't. For a slim girl she filled out the jeans just fine.

"I guess I was just desperate," she said finally.

"Why?"

"Well," she said, "I was twenty-six, and I was working in the saloon. I hated it there. Then Henry walked in. That was five years ago."

That made her thirty-one. He'd thought her a few years older than that. Being married to Henry Miles was already starting to take its toll on her.

"He took me out of there."

"And put you in his café," Clint said. "All he wanted was someone to work for him who he wouldn't have to pay."

"I know that, now."

"Then why not leave him?"

"I can't."

"You don't love him, do you?"

"No."

"Then leave him."

"I can't," she said, hugging her arms as if she were cold. "I'm afraid."

"Afraid of what?"

"I don't know," she said. "Of being alone."

"You won't be alone," he said. "You're pretty enough to get any man you want. You don't have to settle for a Henry Miles, who mistreats you."

"He's my husband—"

He took her by the shoulders and said, "He doesn't deserve you."

"Clint," she said, "I told you I worked in a saloon, but I never—I was never—"

"Are you trying to tell me that all saloon girls aren't whores?"

She nodded.

"I know that, Gena," he said. "I know you were never a whore. But tell me, were you ever really a wife? Has he ever been a real husband to you?"

"You mean, have we ever—"

"Yes, that's what I mean."

"Well, of course we have," she said, "but to tell you the truth, I've never liked it very much."

"Maybe you just have never done it right," he said.

Holding her by the shoulders, he pulled her to him and kissed her. Her lips were stiff for a moment, but then they softened. He used his tongue to open her mouth, and the kiss deepened. When it ended, she was breathless.

"I've . . . never been kissed . . . like that before," she said.

"Well, you should be," he said, "and often."

"Would you—can we do it again?"

He answered by kissing her again. This time she was eager, putting her arms around him, and pressing tightly against him. He reached between them, opened her shirt, and put his hands on her breasts. They were small but firm, and her nipples came to life in his palms. He broke the kiss, ran his lips over her neck and down to her breasts, where he nibbled on her nipples while she sighed and moaned with pleasure.

He slid the shirt off of her completely and then lowered her to the ground, where he finished undressing her. . . .

Later, she lay in the crook of his arm and said, "It's never been like that—not with anyone, but for sure not with Henry. We only do it every so often, and then he just pushes it in me, ruts like a bull, and then rolls off. I've never felt anything, let alone something like I just felt with you."

She looked up at him and asked, "Is it always that good?"

"Not always," he said, kissing her. She looked disappointed and he added, "Sometimes it's better."

"Could we do it again?" she asked.

"Don't you have to get back?" he asked.

She wrapped her hand around his semierect penis and said, "So I'll get back a little late."

As he took her in his arms and she slid atop him he couldn't help marvel at the fact that she was already showing more courage.

THREE

After that was when she talked about babies.

"Have you ever thought about babies?" she asked.

"Not often," he said. "It's not something a man thinks about when he moves around as much as I do."

"Have you ever thought about settling down?"

He smiled and said, "Too late for that, darlin'."

"I want to have babies."

"Then have them," he said.

"Not with Henry," she said. "He hates children. He would be a terrible father."

"Then have them with someone else."

"You?"

"No, not me."

"You would be a wonderful father."

"No, I wouldn't," he said, "because I would never be there. Find yourself a good man, Gena, and have your babies, and a lot of them."

"I'd have to leave Henry for that."

"Then do it."

"And leave Sutter."

"Do that, too."

She sat up, shaking her head.

"I'd have to work up the nerve to do that."

"Then do it."

She looked at him over her shoulder.

"Will you be here to help me?"

"No," he said, "I can't, honey. I have to leave in the morning."

"Oh."

He ran his hand down the line of her back and said, "See what I mean about not being there when you need me?"

She lay back down on the grass next to him and said, "Oh, no, you don't. You were here just when I needed you, and I thank you for it."

"We'd better get back to town," he said.

They got up and dressed, and as they prepared to mount their horses she said, "You never did tell me what Martha said about me."

"Mount up," he said, "and I'll tell you on the way back to town."

Clint left Sutter the next morning without ever seeing Gena again. He wondered if she would actually work up the nerve to leave Henry Miles. He hoped she would. He had the feeling she'd make a wonderful mother to a whole passel of kids.

It was two days later, about half a day's ride from Texas, that he found the baby.

FOUR

Clint spotted the coach from a hilltop and frowned. It was just sitting out in the middle of nowhere, with no one around. The funny thing was, he could hear a lamb bleating in the distance.

Or was it a lamb?

He started down the hill toward the coach, and the bleating got louder and more insistent. Also, it stopped sounding like a sheep. Now it sounded more like . . . a baby.

He gave the reins a quick flick to quicken the team's pace. How could there be a baby in a stagecoach, all by itself?

When he reached the coach he rode his wagon over as close to it as he could and looked inside. The crying was loud and constant. The baby, on the floor of the coach, was covered by a blanket. It was as if someone were trying to hide it.

Clint didn't know quite what to do about the

baby, so he decided first to look at the coach and the surrounding area to see if he could determine what had happened.

He stepped down from his rig and look around. The ground around the coach was covered with tracks made by people and by horses. From the looks of things the only way he could reconstruct the events was that the coach was stopped by riders, and the passengers were made to step out. Whoever the baby had been traveling with must have hidden it under the blanket before stepping down. Now the question was: Where were the people? They couldn't have walked away, leaving the baby behind, so they must have been taken away. Who robs a stage and steals the people?

He climbed up on top of the stage to look for any signs of violence, but there were none. It seemed to have been taken without a struggle.

His examination of the outside of the stage and the immediate area complete, it was time to turn his attention to the baby itself.

He opened the door of the stage and stepped inside. The crying was so loud that it seemed to echo in his head. He pushed back the blanket and looked at the baby. It was red in the face, and its pink little mouth was wide open as it cried. He wondered how long it had been crying and how much longer it could continue. Just looking, he couldn't tell how old the baby was, or whether it was a boy or a girl. The only thing he knew was that it was too young to walk, or fend for itself. He didn't know anything about babies, but he knew he couldn't leave the child here—and that meant he had to pick it up. He hoped he could do that without dropping the little tyke on its head.

After several false starts he managed to get the baby into his arms. He'd been hoping that picking it up would shut it up, but it didn't work that way. The child just kept on crying. He tried rocking, and shaking, and then talking to it, but none of that worked. Then he decided the baby must be hungry. But what did he have to feed to a baby? He certainly couldn't give it any beef jerky, and he couldn't make it some coffee.

He sat in the coach, holding the baby and racking his brain for something he could give to quiet it. The crying was starting to give him a headache. Finally he came up with an idea. The only thing he had that you could reasonably give to a baby was water.

Holding the child in one hand he got out of the coach, walked over to his wagon, and climbed into the back. Inside, the wooden walls were covered with guns, and with equipment for working on guns. He pulled together a couple of blankets to give the baby something soft to lie on, and set it down. He picked up a water canteen and started looking around for a cup. After he poured a little water into a cup he realized the baby couldn't drink from a cup like an adult would. He searched for something else, but he had nothing. Finally he pulled out a clean neckerchief and dipped it in the water. Maybe the child would be satisfied to suck the water from the cloth. He was gratified to see that as soon as the damp cloth touched the child's lips, it opened its mouth and started to suck.

At last the crying stopped. Now maybe he'd be able to think straight.

The question now was: What to do with the baby? Should he take it with him to Texas and drop it off in the first town he came to? Maybe something in the coach would tell him where the baby was headed.

He took the cloth from the baby, and it started to cry again. He dipped the cloth into the water to freshen it and gave it to the baby. Its little hands came up and grabbed it and stuffed it into its mouth. He decided that he could leave the child alone for a short time, just while he searched the interior of the coach.

Inside the coach he looked around, hoping to find something helpful, but there was nothing there. He climbed up onto the top where the luggage was and started going through the bags. He found a bag with some baby clothes, so he dropped down from the coach with it and took it to his rig. Inside, the baby was still sucking on the cloth. He freshened it again and gave it back to the child before it could cry much more, then he started a thorough search of the bag. He was rewarded by a letter, which had apparently been written to the baby's mother from her sister. That meant that the letter was written by the child's aunt. The letter had been mailed from Doyle, Kansas. He had never heard of that town.

He read the letter but was not encouraged. The aunt, whose name was Loretta Kane, was telling her sister—Sally Rise—not to come to Doyle with the baby. She told her sister to stay in the East with her recently departed husband's family, that there was no reason for her to come to Doyle. Apparently, Sally had not heeded her sister's advice and had decided to make the trip anyway.

"So," he said, looking down at the child, "your daddy died and your mommy decided to come West. Now your mommy is missing."

He freshened the cloth again and decided that this would be the last one he would give the baby. He didn't know about small children, but horses didn't fare well when they drank too much water.

"I guess the only thing to do is take you to your aunt. Maybe your mommy will show up there."

He'd take the baby to the nearest town now, get it some milk, and send a telegram to Loretta Kane in Doyle. Maybe she'd be able to come for the baby and would save him a trip to Doyle—wherever that was.

FIVE

The last town Clint had encountered was Tyler Falls. He hadn't spent more than an hour there, and now he was going back to give it a second chance to impress him.

He drove his rig into town and headed straight to the livery stable. He hadn't been to the stable the first time, because he'd only stopped to pick up some supplies and have a drink.

"Didn't I see this rig in town yesterday?" the liveryman asked.

"Yes, I was here for about an hour."

The man opened his mouth and cackled. He was only about fifty, but he had no teeth at all. His gums reminded Clint of the baby.

"Guess you just had to come back, huh?"

"Yup," Clint said, "just had to. You know anyone in town who has a baby?"

"A baby?" the man said. "I don't know of anybody

in town. A couple of ranchers' wives have babies."

"Do you know any women in town who have had kids?"

"Sure, lots of women have had kids. Why?"

At that moment the baby started crying in the back of Clint's rig.

"What's that?"

"That," Clint said, "is a baby."

"A baby? In the back of your rig?"

"That's right."

Clint started walking to the back of the rig to get the baby.

"Hey," the liveryman said, "if'n you intend to leave that baby here, you're gonna have to pay extra."

He opened his toothless mouth and started cackling again.

Clint carried the baby with him to the sheriff's office. If the sheriff was surprised to see a man holding a baby enter his office, he didn't show it.

"Sheriff?"

"That's right," the lawman said. "Sheriff Tom Bush. Can I help you?"

The sheriff was in his thirties, a tall, slender man with an easygoing manner.

Clint explained to the sheriff about finding the coach, deserted except for the baby he was holding.

"What stage line?"

"The writing on the stage was faded," Clint said. "I got the impression it was old, though. It was probably a private stage line with an old, used coach."

"Know where it was headed?"

"Not exactly," Clint said, "but I found a letter that indicated that the baby and its mother were headed for a town called Doyle."

"Doyle," the sheriff said, "is two counties from here. If the stage was headed there it would have had to make at least one stop in between."

"I see. Have you had a rash of stage robberies hereabouts?"

"No," the sheriff said, "this is the first one."

"And the last, I hope," Clint said.

The baby made a sound then, and started crying.

"He sounds hungry," Bush said. "Is it a boy or a girl?"

Clint laughed and said, "I don't know, but it sure does cry a lot."

Bush came closer and looked at the baby.

"Hungry," he said.

"I know," Clint said. "All I was able to give it was water. Do you know where I can get some milk?"

"You'll need someone to feed it, too," the sheriff said. He grabbed his hat and said, "Come on."

"Where?"

"My house," the sheriff said. "My wife will welcome the opportunity to hold and feed a baby."

SIX

Margaret Bush was delighted to take the baby from Clint's arms.

"Is it a boy or a girl?" she asked, cradling the baby.

"I don't know, ma'am."

"Didn't you bother to look?"

"Ma'am?"

"Look, all you had to do was look," she said. "Oh, men. Come along, darling," she said to the baby. "We're going to feed you, and wash you, and change you." Over her shoulder she called, "Tom, you give Mr. Adams a cup of coffee. There's a fresh pot on the stove."

"You heard my orders, Mr. Adams. Coffee?"

"I reckon I can use one."

"Come on into the kitchen."

Clint followed the sheriff into the kitchen. The man poured two cups and set them on the table.

"Have a seat, Mr. Adams."

"Sheriff," Clint said, "you and your wife are doing me a big favor. I wish you would call me Clint."

"All right, Clint. What are you planning to do now?"

"Well, I've got that letter from the baby's aunt. I figured to send her a telegram, see if she won't come and pick up the baby."

"And if she won't?"

"I'll have to go to Doyle myself and bring the baby to her."

"And if she doesn't want it?"

"I don't know, Sheriff," Clint said. "I guess I'll have to figure that out when the time comes. I better go and send that telegram. Thanks for the coffee. I'll check back in a little while about the baby."

"Maybe by then," the sheriff said, "we'll know whether it's a boy or a girl."

"It'll be nice to think of that baby as something other than 'it,' " Clint said.

"Wait up," the sheriff said. "I've got to go back to my office, so I might as well walk you to the telegraph office."

When they reached the telegraph office Clint thanked the sheriff again and told him he'd see him later.

Clint went inside to send the telegram to Loretta Kane, but when he had the pencil in his hand he had a problem composing it. Quickly, he decided to send the telegram and address it to the sheriff of the town of Doyle. Let the sheriff break the news to Loretta Kane in person. It might lessen the shock.

He related the problem in as few words as possible, then handed the telegram to the clerk and paid the fee.

"You gonna wait for an answer?" the clerk asked.

"No," Clint said.

"Be at the hotel?"

"Uh, I guess so," Clint said. "If you don't find me, bring the answer to the sheriff."

"Yes, sir."

Clint left the office and walked back to the livery to pick up his gear, which he took with him to the hotel.

Once he had his gear stowed in a room he decided to take a leisurely bath. Maybe soaking in some hot water would relax not only his body but his mind as well.

George Proctor had been the sheriff of Doyle for the past ten years. He knew Loretta Kane well. She had come to Doyle seven years ago as a twenty-year-old kid who was already somewhat jaded. The telegram in his hand was a surprise to him. He never knew that Loretta had a sister, and now he had to tell her that her sister was missing. He wondered how twenty-seven-year-old Loretta would react to the fact that there was a baby who needed a home . . . and she was the only relative.

"Forget it," Loretta said.

"Loretta," Proctor said, "this baby is your blood."

"George," she said, putting her hands on her hips, "do I look like someone who could take care of a baby?"

They were in her room upstairs from the saloon,

where she worked. The dress she wore was cut low to reveal the creamy swell of her breasts. Proctor, at thirty-eight, was hopelessly in love with Loretta Kane. If he had his way they'd have been married a long time ago, but whenever he approached her with the subject she always used the same two words: "Forget it!"

"Loretta," he said, "she's your sister—"

"And I haven't seen her in over ten years," Loretta said. "Look, George, I gotta get back to work. You brought me the message and I appreciate it, but there's nothing I can do."

"Just answer the telegram, then," he said, offering it to her.

She waved her hand and said, "It's addressed to you. I got to get back downstairs, or I'll get fired."

As she left the room, George knew she could never get fired. The owner of the Bull's-eye Saloon, Victor Ward, was in love with her, too.

Shaking his head sadly, George Proctor left the saloon and went back to the telegraph office to send Clint Adams his answer.

SEVEN

Clint was in the saloon when Sheriff Bush found him. As the lawman walked in, Clint got an attack of the guilts. Here he was, having a drink, when the sheriff's wife was minding the baby for him.

"Sheriff," he said, "I was, uh, just having a drink before coming over to see you."

"Relax, Clint," Bush said. "Nobody's rushing you, least of all my wife. I'll have a drink with you."

The bartender came over and poured the sheriff a whiskey.

"I got your answer from Doyle," Bush said, taking the telegram out of his pocket with one hand while holding his drink with the other.

"Bad?" Clint asked.

"You ain't gonna be happy."

Clint accepted the telegram and read it. The sheriff of Doyle, a man named Proctor, said that Loretta Kane regretted that she could be of no help.

"That's it?" Clint said. "She regrets she can be of no help?"

Bush shrugged and sipped his drink.

"I can't accept this," Clint said, dropping the telegram on the bar.

"Why not?"

"Loretta Kane is this baby's blood," Clint said. "My God, the woman's sister is missing. Doesn't she have any feelings?"

"Maybe not," Bush said. "This means you're going to Doyle?"

"I have to."

"With the baby?"

"What else can I do?"

Bush sipped his drink again and then set it down. "Leave her with us."

"Her?"

"Yup," Bush said, "the baby is a girl."

"Leave her with you?"

"Sure," Bush said. "My wife would love to have her."

"That wouldn't be right."

"Why not?"

"We don't know that the baby's mother is dead," Clint said. "If I left the baby with you, your wife would fall in love with her."

"She already has."

"Then what happens when the mother shows up?" Clint asked. "What would that do to your wife?"

Bush frowned and said, "You're right . . . but what happens if you go to Doyle and the sister still refuses to help?"

"While I'm in Doyle," Clint said, "you'll be here

trying to find out what happened to the sister. If we both come up empty, I'll come back here with the baby, and you can take the proper steps to adopt her."

"That sounds fair."

"There's only one thing, Sheriff," Clint said, "and you may want to hit me after I've said this, but—"

The sheriff raised his hand and said, "I know what you're going to say. I'd better do my damndest to find out what happened, so it doesn't come back and bite me on the ass later."

Clint stared at the man, impressed by him.

"You've thought this through, haven't you?"

"Thoroughly."

"Well," Clint said, "I'll leave in the morning."

"Will you leave the baby with us overnight?"

"If you don't think it would be too hard on your wife to let her go in the morning."

"I think it would be better for the baby."

"So do I," Clint said. "Can you tell me where I can get a good steak around here?"

"Sure can," the sheriff said with a smile. "My house."

"Sheriff, I don't want to impose on your wife—"

"It was her idea," the sheriff said. "Dinner's at seven. All right?"

"I'll be there."

Dinner was very good, and Clint told Margaret Bush so. She smiled at his praise and shooed them out into the living room to have their coffee.

"I've got to prepare the baby's bottle."

In the living room Clint said, "I don't know how I'm going to keep up with its—uh, her feedings."

"Margaret has made up a schedule and written it out for you," Bush said.

"That's kind of her."

"She also managed to rustle up a couple of bottles to take with you. The only thing we can't give you is milk. It will go bad. You'll have to find that along the way."

"I don't think that will be a problem."

"I don't see why it would be," Bush said. "Even the coldest heart can be melted by a child."

Thinking about Loretta Kane, Clint said, "I hope you're right."

In the morning Clint checked out of the hotel, collected Duke and his rig from the livery, then drove over to the Bush house to collect the baby. They were waiting for him.

Margaret Bush carried the baby out and placed her in the back of the rig herself, making sure the child was safe and comfortable.

"Good-bye, little darling," Clint heard her say. She kissed the baby and then dropped down from the rig with Clint's help.

"You take good care of that child, Clint Adams, do you hear me?"

Margaret hugged Clint and kissed him on the cheek.

"God bless you, Clint, for being the man you are."

Tom Bush came over, shook hands with Clint, and then put his arm around his wife and led her back to the house. They waved to Clint and watched him until he disappeared around the bend.

Clint looked behind him to make sure the baby

was all right. He wasn't sure he was doing the right thing. Tom and Margaret Bush would obviously have given the child a loving home, but if and when the mother showed up it would tear Margaret's heart out to give her up. An aunt would realize that the situation could be temporary, and an aunt was a blood relative and *should* give the child a good home if the mother didn't return, or turned up dead.

In the case of Loretta Kane, though, this might not be the case. At least Clint had to give it a try. He felt very strongly that this was something he had to do.

EIGHT

Clint made one stop between Tyler Falls and Doyle, and he had no trouble getting some milk for the baby from a matronly woman who ran a café there. The woman said she had three grown children of her own, and she would give Clint all the milk he wanted.

Toward evening, the second day after leaving Tyler Falls, Clint drove his rig into Doyle, Kansas. He took the rig directly to the livery, and carried the baby right to the sheriff's office.

"Sheriff Proctor?" he asked, entering the office.

"In a minute," the man in the office said. He walked into the back and Clint heard a cell door open. "All right, Harry, get out, time to go home."

"I thought you was gonna hang me, Sheriff," another voice said.

"We stopped hanging people for breaking windows, Harry," the sheriff said.

The two men came into sight, and the lawman

walked a frail-looking man in his fifties to the door.

"Go home, Harry, and stay out of trouble."

"I always try, Sheriff."

"Try harder," the sheriff said, and closed the door.

"Sheriff Proctor?" Clint said again.

"Yeah, that's me," Proctor said. He turned and looked at Clint for the first time and noticed the baby. "You're Adams?"

"That's right."

"I sent you a telegram telling you not to come, Mr. Adams," Proctor said.

"That's not exactly true, Sheriff," Clint said. "You said that Loretta Kane said she couldn't help me."

"Same thing."

"I came to try to change her mind."

"I seriously doubt that you can do that, Mr. Adams," the lawman said, seating himself behind his desk.

"Maybe I can't," Clint said, "but perhaps this baby can."

Proctor seemed reluctant to look at the child Clint held in his arms.

"Will you take me to Loretta Kane, Sheriff?"

"Not with that baby in your arms," the sheriff said, pointing.

"Why not?"

"Because Loretta Kane works at the saloon, Mr. Adams," Proctor said, "and a saloon is no place for a baby. Would you agree with that?"

"I guess I'd have to," Clint said. "I'm going over to the hotel, Sheriff. I'm going to need someone to look after this baby while I go and talk to her aunt, Miss Kane."

Proctor frowned and tapped his fingers on the top of his desk.

"All right, Adams," he said finally. "There's a woman here in town who does a lot of baby-sitting. I'll talk to her and see if she's available. If she is, I'll send her to you at the hotel."

"I'd be very grateful for that, Sheriff."

"Well, I'm gonna give you some advice that you should be grateful for as well, Mr. Adams."

"I always listen to advice, Sheriff."

"You can talk to Loretta Kane, but once she tells you how she feels, I don't want you badgering her."

"Is that advice, Sheriff?" Clint asked. "Or is that a warning?"

"You can take it as whatever you like," Proctor said, "as long as you remember it."

"I'll remember it, Sheriff," Clint said. As small as the baby was, his arm was starting to ache from holding her. "Could you direct me to the hotel?"

"You can't miss it," the lawman said. "Go out and turn left, and just keep walking."

The last line sounded like something the sheriff fervently wished Clint Adams would do.

NINE

Clint was in his hotel room with the baby for half an hour before there was a knock on the door. When he opened the door a portly white-haired woman was standing in the hallway.

"Are you the man with the baby?" she asked.

"That's right," Clint said. "I have to—"

"Where's your wife, young man?" she asked.

"I don't have a wife, ma'am," Clint said.

"Then where did you get a baby?"

"I found it."

"Found it?"

"Would you like to come in, ma'am?"

"Of course," she said. "How can I care for the baby if I don't come in?"

He stepped back and allowed her to enter. She went right to the baby, who was lying on the bed.

"A girl, right?"

"Yes, ma'am."

"Stop calling me 'ma'am,' " the woman said. "My name is Mrs. Gordon."

"Mrs. Gordon," he said. "I have to—"

"What a beauty she is," Mrs. Gordon said. "You know, you shouldn't leave her on the bed like this. She could roll off and get hurt."

"I'm sorry, ma—I'm sorry, Mrs. Gordon. I'm really not very good at taking care of a baby."

Mrs. Gordon took the pillow from the bed and tucked the pillow under the mattress on one side. She then went to the other side, took the blanket from the bed, and tucked it under the mattress on the other side.

"Now, you see? Both ends of the mattress are lifted, and she can't roll off."

"I see."

"Well, how long will you need me for?"

"Uh, I'm not sure," Clint said. "Certainly a couple of hours. I need to get something to eat, and then talk to the baby's aunt."

"Where is the mother?"

"She is missing, Mrs. Gordon," Clint said, and explained the whole story to her.

"The poor thing," Mrs. Gordon said. She picked the baby up and cradled her in her arms. "You poor little thing. Don't you worry, Sadie is gonna take good care of you."

"I got a couple of bottles of milk from downstairs," Clint said. "The hotel dining room was nice enough to give me some."

"The least they could do," Mrs. Gordon said. "All right, Mr. . . ."

"Adams."

"Mr. Adams," she said, "you go and eat and do

what you have to do. This beautiful little girl and I will be just fine."

"I appreciate this, Mrs. Gordon," Clint said.

"Don't appreciate it," she said. "It's not a favor. You'll be paying me for this."

"And you'll be worth every penny," he said. "I can tell."

"Oh, get out," she told him, "and remember one thing: I'm watching this child so you can do what you have to do, and not so you can go to the saloon to drink and play poker. Understand?"

"Mrs. Gordon," Clint said, trying to sound as sincere as possible, "I understand perfectly."

Clint found a small café and had a steak with onions and potatoes. During dinner he went over in his mind how he would approach the reluctant aunt, Loretta Kane. He tried five or ten different ones, but none of them seemed to work for him. He finally decided that he was simply going to have to be straightforward about it.

After dinner he went to the sheriff's office and found the man behind his desk, drinking coffee.

"Did Mrs. Gordon get over to the hotel?" the lawman asked.

"Yes, thanks," Clint said. "Are you ready to take me to see Loretta Kane?"

"Sure," Proctor said. He put the coffee cup down on the desk and stood up. "I'd rather have a beer right now than coffee, anyway."

Clint felt like having a beer or two himself, but he remembered Mrs. Gordon's warning.

They stepped outside, and Clint followed the sheriff's lead.

"You know," Proctor said, "she may not want to talk to you at all."

"I realize that."

"And I won't be able to force her to."

"I know that, also."

"Just as long as you know."

From the two conversations he'd had with Sheriff George Proctor, Clint had a feeling that the lawman not only knew Loretta Kane, but also knew her quite well.

TEN

Sheriff George Proctor took Clint to the Bull's-eye Saloon. It was an impressive setup, with maximum use of space to get a lot of tables into the center of the room, as well as gaming tables against the walls all around the room. Clint mentioned this, and Proctor nodded.

"You should have seen this place before Vic Ward came here from San Francisco five years ago and bought it."

"*From* San Francisco *to* here?"

"I know," Proctor said, "it sounds unusual, but Ward said he was tired of the high life in San Francisco and decided to come here to get away from it. Come on, let's get a beer."

They walked to the bar, where things were elbow to elbow, but when men saw that it was the sheriff, they shifted to make room.

When they each had a beer in hand, Clint turned

and looked at the room. There were three women working the room and they were all stunning, but he especially noticed the one with red hair.

"Is Loretta Kane in the room?" he asked.

"I don't see her now," Proctor said, "but then Loretta makes her own hours."

"I guess she must be pretty popular."

"Very," Proctor said, and Clint thought he could read a lot into that single word.

Clint was about to ask when he could talk to her when a well-dressed man in his forties approached them.

"Sheriff," the man said, "a little early for you tonight, isn't it?"

"A little, Vic," Proctor said. "I'd like you to meet Clint Adams. He just rode into town today."

Ward looked delighted.

"I know Mr. Adams by reputation," Ward said, extending his hand. Clint shook it. Ward looked at the bartender and shook his head. Clint assumed that meant they would not be charged for the drinks.

"Thank you," Clint said, raising the mug.

"Would you care to do some gambling?" Ward asked. "I have some of the very best dealers in the business."

Clint smiled and asked, "Is that supposed to tempt me, Mr. Ward?"

Ward laughed.

"Mr. Adams isn't here to gamble, Vic," Proctor said. "He's here to see Loretta."

"Loretta?" Ward said, frowning now. "How do you know Loretta?"

"I don't," Clint said. "I've never met the lady."

"Then what business do you have with her?" Ward demanded.

Clint was going to tell him, but then changed his mind.

"That's between the lady and me, I'm afraid," Clint said. "Where is she, please?"

"I'm afraid you can't see her," Ward said.

"Why not?"

"Because—"

"Let him see her, Vic."

Ward glared at Proctor and said, "Why should I?"

"Because he has business with her," Proctor said. "It has to do with her family."

"What family?"

"I'll let her tell you that, Mr. Ward, after I talk to her," Clint said, and then added, "that is, if she wants to share it with you."

"Of course she'll share it with me," Ward said. He glared at Proctor but continued speaking to Clint. "Who else would she share it with?"

The look told Clint a lot. Both of these men were in love with Loretta Kane, and competing for her. He certainly didn't want to step into the middle of a love triangle.

"Look," Clint said, "just tell me where she is and let me talk to her. I'm sure the rest of this can be straightened out later."

"I'm not just going to let him see her," Ward said, stubbornly. "I'm going to talk to her first. If she wants to see him, that's another matter."

This was rapidly becoming harder than it should have been.

Proctor looked at Clint and shrugged.

"All right," Clint said, "I'll wait."

"Have another beer, on the house," Ward said, and walked away. Clint watched as he walked to a stairway at the back of the room and went up.

"He's a hardnose," Proctor said. "We might as well drink his beer."

Clint put the empty mug on the bar so it could be refilled.

"Look," he said to Proctor, "you and Ward seem to think an awful lot of Miss Kane—"

"We do."

"I'm not trying to hurt her," Clint said, "I'm just trying to do the best I can for the baby."

"The best you could have done for the baby," Proctor said, "was not to bring her here."

"I'm sorry," Clint said, "but that baby has a relative here. Even if she doesn't want it, she can tell me where I can find other relatives."

Proctor thought that over and nodded.

"I can understand that."

"Good," Clint said. "Then use your influence on Ward to make this a little easier on all of us."

"What makes you think I have any influence with Vic Ward?"

"Well, you seem to be friendly—"

"That's all on the surface," Proctor said. "I respect the man, but as you said, we both think a lot of Loretta Kane. We're not friends, and to tell you the truth, I don't think we ever will be."

Clint was about to say something else when he saw Ward coming down the steps. The man's face was set hard as he approached.

"Well?" Clint asked.

"She doesn't want to see you, Mr. Adams," Ward said.

"Now, look—" Clint said.

"You are free to stay here and drink or gamble," Ward said, "but if you try to see her, if you try to go up those stairs, I will have you shot."

He raised his arm, and Clint saw two men wearing guns move forward from their posts in two different corners of the room.

"You're making this much harder than it should be," Clint said.

"If it is going to be hard on anyone," Ward said, "it will be you. I promise you that."

Clint looked at Sheriff Proctor, who shrugged his shoulders.

"I told you," Proctor said, "that I couldn't, and wouldn't, force her to see you."

"I'm telling you both right now," Clint said, angrily looking at them both in turn, "I will see her before I leave town. That's a promise."

Clint turned and left the saloon.

ELEVEN

As Clint left, Proctor and Ward exchanged a glance.

"We both know his reputation," Proctor said. "That is not a good man to have mad at you."

"I don't care," Ward said. "Gunsmith or not, he doesn't tell me what to do in my own place. You're the sheriff, Proctor, you better get him to leave town."

"I feel the same way you do, Vic," Proctor said. "Nobody tells me how to do my job." He put his beer mug down, preparing to leave, and said, "That includes you."

Upstairs, Loretta Kane was nursing a swelling on her upper cheek. She hoped it wouldn't bruise. Damn Vic Ward and his quick hands, anyway. All she'd said was that maybe she should talk to the man if he came all this way. If she wasn't so afraid of Vic, she'd leave the saloon and leave town. But where would she go? She couldn't go back East, she'd never do that. If only Sally had listened and stayed where she was safe. The stage she'd been on had probably been robbed, and Sally had probably been taken. Thank God the baby was safe, but what the hell was she gonna do with a baby in a saloon? That was crazy. Vic was right: If she didn't talk to the man at all, then maybe he'd turn around and go back where he came from.

She leaned closer to the mirror. Was her cheek bruising? Damn Vic Ward, she said, as she prepared to cover the bruise with makeup. . . .

Vic Ward glared at the door Clint Adams and George Proctor had used. He stared until the batwing doors stopped swinging.

"Want a beer, Vic?" the bartender asked.

Vic glared at the bartender, who backed off and walked away. When his boss had that look on his face he didn't want to be anywhere near him.

Ward turned away from the bar and walked to the back of the room, where there was a curtained doorway. He went through, turned left, and walked down the hall to a door that led to his office. Inside, he poured himself a brandy and sat down behind his desk. It was bad enough that he had to compete with George Proctor for Loretta, now he was going to have to keep her away from Clint Adams and that goddamn baby. That's all a woman needed to change her way of thinking, was a baby.

Vic Ward would kill Loretta Kane before he'd let her get away from him.

• • •

Shannon had been watching Vic Ward and Sheriff Proctor talk with the stranger. The man had attracted her attention as soon as he entered. He wasn't any handsomer than any other man, but there was something in the way he carried himself that made a woman notice him. Shannon knew that the other girls, Stacy and Tina, had noticed him, too. Once, Shannon saw him looking at her, but then Vic had joined the stranger and the sheriff at the bar. At first they had seemed friendly, but then things turned ugly. Shannon got close enough to them to hear Loretta's name. It seemed that the stranger wanted to see Loretta, and naturally Vic didn't like that. Vic didn't like anyone seeing Loretta unless he said so. It was funny, he would let her work the room, teasing the customers, even sitting in their laps, but he'd kill any man who tried to see her in private. Sheriff Proctor was about the only man Shannon knew of who could talk to Loretta without having to go up against Vic, and that was probably only because he was the law. Now there was this stranger, and both Proctor and Vic Ward seemed to respect him some.

She wondered who the stranger was and why he wanted to see Loretta.

Shannon knew that she was nosy, but she couldn't help it. Plus, she was interested in the stranger, so she decided to do a little snooping around to see if she could find out what was going on.

Walking back to the hotel, Clint found he was angrier than he had been in a long time. He just wasn't sure who he was angry at.

He could have been angry at Proctor for not giving him more help.

Or it could have been Vic Ward, who was being so hardnosed about letting him talk to Loretta. Clint wasn't all that sure that Loretta was the one who didn't want him to see her.

Beyond that he was probably angry at himself for getting involved in this thing—but he couldn't have left that baby out there by herself. Maybe he should have left the baby with Tom and Margaret Bush and washed his hands of the whole thing.

He thought briefly of the night he had spent in the wagon with the baby. At one point the poor little thing cried out in her sleep and seemed to be twitching. Clint had picked her up and held her, and that seemed to calm her down. He laid down with her and spent the rest of the night being careful not to roll over on her. Lying with her like that he felt real close to her, and he had vowed to do his damndest to see that she ended up in a good home if her mother didn't return.

He didn't think living with Loretta Kane over a saloon was a good home, but he still felt that he had to talk to the baby's blood kin before he did anything else.

It was going to take more than Vic Ward and his hired bouncers to keep him from seeing Loretta Kane.

Sheriff George Proctor went back to his office. Like Clint, he wasn't so sure that not seeing Adams was Loretta's idea. He decided to talk to Loretta himself tomorrow and see just what the story was. If she didn't want to see Adams, then he'd do his best to see that Adams didn't bother her. If, however, not seeing Adams was Ward's idea, then he'd do what he could to see that Clint Adams and Loretta Kane had a chance to talk.

TWELVE

Clint paid Mrs. Gordon, thanked her, and sent her on her way. He sat on the bed with the baby, who looked happy and content. It was so easy to make a baby happy. When she grew up she would never remember how she'd been left alone in a stagecoach, found by a strange man, and hauled all over the countryside. She'd never remember that she slept in a wagon, and in a hotel bed with a propped-up mattress, she'd never know who Mrs. Gordon was, and if Sally Rise didn't show up, she'd never remember what her real mother looked like.

And she'd never remember a man named Clint Adams.

Clint took off his boots and was about to lie down next to the baby, who had fallen asleep, when there was a knock on the door. He walked to it and opened it. A woman with red hair stood in the hall. She looked familiar.

"Hello," he said.

"Our eyes met across a crowded room," she said.

Now he remembered her from the saloon.

"Actually," he said, leaning against the wall, "they didn't. I saw you, though."

"Good," she said. "My name is Shannon."

"That figures."

She cocked her head to one side and asked, "And why do you say that?"

He smiled and said, "Red hair, face like an angel, little sprinkling of freckles across the bridge of the nose and the cheeks, and eyes like emeralds. Let me guess. You're Irish, right?"

"Right you are, but you didn't mention the body, though." She shot her left hip out to put the body on display.

He studied her for a moment. She was medium height, about five-four, and slender except for her breasts, which were large and round.

"I'll reserve my opinion."

She frowned and said, "Why?"

"Clothes can hide a multitude of sins."

She smiled and said, "If you let me in we could solve that little problem."

"I would," Clint said, "but I have somebody here, and I don't think she wants to get off the bed."

"Oh," Shannon said, looking disappointed. "One of the other girls get here ahead of me? Is it Stacy? Tina?"

"As a matter of fact," Clint said, "I don't even know her name."

"I'll bet it's Tina," Shannon said. "That bitch. She knew—"

"No, it's not Tina," Clint said. "Come on in and I'll introduce you."

He stepped aside to allow her to enter. As soon as she did she saw the baby on the bed.

"Oh, my God," she said, moving to the bed to get a closer look. "She's so beautiful."

"So you see why I can't make her get off the bed," Clint said.

"You bastard," she said, keeping her voice low, "you made me think there was another woman in here."

"Well," he said, "there is another female in here."

"And she's beautiful," Shannon said.

"That makes two of you."

She smiled at him and said, "You're sweet."

She was still wearing her saloon dress, but she had a woolen shawl over her shoulders. It was hiding her cleavage, but it couldn't hide the size of her breasts.

"So now there are two females in here," he said, "and I'd like to know why. Did Vic Ward send you?"

"Vic? No. Why would he send me here?"

"Maybe to distract me," Clint said.

"From what?"

"Or to change my mind."

"About what?"

"About what I came here to do."

"And what might that be?"

"You don't already know?"

She studied him for a few moments and then looked at the baby, still sleeping peacefully on the bed.

"Might it have somethin' to do with this lovely child?" she asked.

"It might."

"Is this child Vic's?"

He laughed and said, "Not hardly."

They faced each other in silence for a few moments and then she said, "All right, then, I'll be totally honest with you."

"Is that something you're used to?"

"Actually, it is," she said. "I came up here on my own because I saw you at the saloon with the sheriff and Vic, and I got curious. It's the devil I carry inside myself that I'm very curious. So I came over here, found out your name from the register, and came up to introduce myself. That's all there is to it, Clint Adams."

"And you have no notion of why I'm here in Doyle?" he asked.

"None at all," she said, "but I was thinkin' I might be able to get you to tell me."

"And why would I do that?"

"Because," she said, "I might be able to help you."

"How?"

"Vic was real upset when you left, and he exchanged some angry-looking words with the sheriff. The only time Vic gets that upset it usually has something to do with Miss Loretta High-and-Mighty Kane."

Clint studied Shannon, wondering if she was just a smart girl who was putting two and two together, or if she was trying to pull the wool over his eyes.

"Wait a minute," she said, her green eyes flashing with excitement, "don't tell me that this child is Loretta Kane's?"

"Not Loretta's," Clint said, "but her sister's."

"And where is her sister?"

"Missing," Clint said. He decided he just might need a friendly hand here in Doyle, and Shannon was apparently extending one. He chose to believe what she said about being here on her own, and told her how he found the baby.

"Poor child," she said, looking at the baby with tenderness.

"You know Loretta, Shannon," Clint said. "I'm wondering if she didn't want to talk to me, or if it was Vic Ward who didn't want her to talk to me."

"I don't know for sure," she said, "but maybe if I told you about her and Vic Ward it might help."

"Sit down," he said, moving a stiff-backed wooden chair to her side of the room. He sat gingerly on the edge of the bed, not wanting to disturb the sleeping child. "Tell me about it."

THIRTEEN

Shannon told Clint that as far as Vic Ward was concerned, he owned Loretta Kane. He didn't feel that way about herself or the other girls, Stacy and Tina, and for that they were grateful. Being "owned" by Vic Ward meant that occasionally you walked around with some bruises on your face.

"He beats her?" he asked in disgust. A man who would strike a woman was almost as bad as a backshooter, as far as he was concerned.

"If he ever touched me," she said, "I'd cut his heart out."

"Why does she put up with it?"

"I've asked myself that often," Shannon said.

"And what answer do you come up with?"

"I think she . . . likes it."

That made Clint's disgust deepen.

"Really?"

"She does whatever he tells her to do, without question."

"I got the impression that the sheriff cared pretty much for her."

"You're right," Shannon said. "In fact, he's the only one who can talk to her outside of the saloon. I don't think Vic wants to tangle with the law."

"And what about Loretta? How does she feel about the sheriff?"

"I think she could love him if she'd let herself, but she's too afraid of Vic and what he might do," she said. "Vic's a real gentleman under most circumstances, except when it comes to Loretta, but he's always got a couple of fellas with guns around."

"Yeah, I saw them."

"I don't suppose they would bother you none, bein' who you are."

"Nobody likes to be outgunned, Shannon," Clint told her. "Do you and Loretta ever talk?"

"Vic lets her out of her room to work the room, and he keeps a sharp eye on her. She hardly ever talks to the rest of us."

"How long has this been going on?"

"I've been here two years," she said. "Tina's been here four, and she says it's been that way since then. Tina's my best friend."

"The bitch?" he asked, and she smiled sheepishly. "Which one is Tina?"

"The long, tall blonde with the tiny, uh, chest and big, wide mouth. You like tall blondes with big mouths, Clint?"

"I like all women, Shannon."

Shannon stood up, looked down at the baby girl on the bed, and said, "I can see that. Well, Mr. Adams, I guess there's a part of my curiosity that isn't goin' to be satisfied tonight."

"There will be other times, Miss Shannon."

"You're not leavin' town?"

He shook his head.

"Not until I talk to Loretta Kane."

"Well," she said, "then I'll be seein' you." She allowed the shawl to slip down her shoulders so he could see that she had some freckles on her pale shoulders, and on the slopes of her firm breasts.

Clint took two steps, grabbed her shoulders, pulled her to him, and kissed her. Her mouth opened beneath his, her tongue hot and darting in his mouth.

"That's for sure, Shannon."

He opened the door for her and she said, "You take good care of that child."

"I will."

She started down the hall and he called out, "Hey, is it Something Shannon, or Shannon Something?"

"It's Shannon, Mr. Adams," she said, over her shoulder, "just Shannon."

FOURTEEN

Vic Ward poured himself his third glass of brandy since his meeting with Clint Adams. More and more he was thinking that he had to get Clint Adams out of town. After all, what woman could resist a baby?

He put his glass down and walked to the office door. He went into the hall, leaving the office door open behind him, and walked down to the curtained doorway. He stuck his head out and caught the attention of one of his men, Danny McGirt.

"Boss?"

"Come into my office."

"Sure, boss," McGirt said. He, in turn, caught the attention of the other man, Sam Downing, who nodded in return, indicating that he understood he'd have the whole room for a while.

By the time McGirt got to the office, Ward was seated behind his desk again.

"Close the door," Ward said.

McGirt obeyed. He had worked for Ward for the past two years. His ostensible job was to keep peace in the saloon, but his true job was to do whatever his boss paid him to do. The other six men who worked for Ward as strong-arm help had all been hired by McGirt.

"Did you see the man I was talking to tonight?" Ward asked. He did not offer McGirt a drink or a seat, but McGirt didn't care about that.

"Yes, sir," McGirt said. "The man who came in with the sheriff."

"That's right," Ward said. "His name is Clint Adams. Does that mean anything to you?"

"No, sir," McGirt said, "unless you're referring to his reputation as the Gunsmith?"

"Of course I'm referring to that, you idiot."

McGirt took the insult with stolid silence. He was a big man in his late twenties, good at his job. If he had wanted he could have broken Victor Ward in half, and Ward was a good-sized man, but that would have cut off McGirt's pipeline to the good life. Victor Ward paid Danny McGirt very well, so McGirt was willing to suffer an insult or two—but not much more than that.

"Are you trying to tell me that his reputation means nothing to you?"

"The Gunsmith's reputation was made a long time ago, Mr. Ward," McGirt said. "He's a dinosaur."

"A dinosaur," Ward said. He sat back and smiled. "I like that."

McGirt did not comment. He waited for his boss to tell him what he wanted done.

"He must have a room over at the hotel," Ward said.

"Yes, sir."

Ward poured himself another brandy while he thought over his options.

"McGirt," he said, finally, "at this time tomorrow night, I don't want Clint Adams to be in Doyle. Do you understand?"

"Let's make it clear, boss," McGirt said. "Do you care how I do it?"

Ward thought that over and then said, "No, McGirt, I don't care how you do it."

McGirt nodded shortly and said, "All right. I'll take care of it."

As McGirt left the office, Ward poured himself another brandy, but held the bottle tipped too long and overflowed the glass. He tried to wipe the excess off the desk with his hand, and then lifted the glass to his mouth, spilling some onto his shirt.

In the hall McGirt briefly flirted with handling Clint Adams himself, but he refused to allow Adams's reputation to affect the way he did things. Better to delegate this job to a couple of the other men. McGirt had picked his men carefully, none of them being over thirty. He didn't think any of them would be influenced by the reputation of Clint Adams, the Gunsmith.

As he reentered the saloon, Tina Blake came over and leaned her arm on his shoulder. McGirt was a solidly built man of five-ten who didn't mind in the least that Tina Blake was six feet tall. For such a tall woman, though, with wide shoulders, she had small breasts.

"Gonna be busy tonight, Danny?" she asked.

"Not too busy for you, honey." He moved his hand around and laid it on her butt. She had a high, firm ass and long, limber legs. More than once he'd thought that if she had her friend Shannon's tits, she'd be almost perfect. "I'll see you after closing."

"Your place or mine?" she asked, dazzling him with her smile. She had the widest, sexiest mouth he had ever seen.

"Mine, darlin'," he said, "and I mean *right* after closing."

"I'll be there."

He looked around the room and asked, "Where's Shannon?"

"She said she had an errand to run," Tina said. "She'll be right back."

"Do me a favor, honey," he said.

"Sure, Dan."

"Find me Eddie Drake, okay? Tell him I want to see him now."

"Sure, Danny, honey," Tina said. "My pleasure."

"No, Tina," he said, pinching her firm butt, "that comes tonight."

FIFTEEN

The baby was the first female Clint had ever shared a bed with where he had to be careful not to roll over on her. He didn't really mind, though. The one problem he thought he might be having was that she would the first female in a long time whose company he didn't want to give up. He was in danger of doing what he thought Margaret Bush might do. He was in danger of falling in love with this tiny little person. He didn't even mind changing her when she was wet—or worse—the way Margaret had shown him how.

He was wide awake now, looking down at her as she slept. He felt that all he had to do was get Loretta Kane to look at the baby, and she'd feel what everyone else who had seen her felt. At that point, if she didn't want to take the baby herself, she could tell him who in the family would.

He heard a floorboard creak, which could have

meant anything. Even though it was late, plenty of men would be coming back from the saloon after closing. Still, he chose to play it carefully, and got up from the bed, gun in hand. It was then he heard a sound outside his window, where there was a low roof. Normally he did not accept rooms with a low roof outside the window, but his concern this time had been for the baby, and he had not asked for a change of rooms.

Hurriedly, he pulled the pillow from underneath the mattress and set it down in a corner of the room. He picked the baby up from the bed and laid her down on the pillow, then picked up the chair and placed it in front of her, lying on its side, and then draped a blanket over it. In effect, the baby was now inside a small tent. He hoped this would afford her enough protection against whatever was to come.

Clint walked over to the window and stood alongside it, his back to the wall. From this position he could cover both the window and the door. A situation like this, if the men were pros, was usually well timed for two men to enter the room together, by the window and the door. Clint didn't see how he could thwart this attempt at him without shots being fired, and that would definitely distress the baby. He was going to have to dispatch his attackers as quickly as possible and get to the baby to calm her down.

In bed with Tina Blake, Dan McGirt heard the shots being fired from the hotel.

Tina Blake lifted her head up from between his legs and said, "What was that?"

"Nothin', honey," he assured her. He put his

hands on her head and pushed her back down to him. "Just keep doin' what you're doin'."

She allowed him to lower her head, opened her wide mouth, and took him inside again.

The door exploded inward a split second before the window broke. Their timing was off just that much, and that was all Clint needed. There was even more of a giveaway than that, however. Just before the door opened, Clint noticed through the crack underneath it that the light in the hall had been extinguished. Thus he was prepared when the door slammed open from a powerful kick.

Since it was already dark in the room, he had no trouble making out the shape in the doorway. He fired, and as the bullet slammed into the attacker, the man's finger jerked on the trigger of his own gun, firing it once.

As the window shattered, Clint swung his gun backhanded and struck someone a blow across the face. The man grunted and fell backward. Clint turned around and fired a shot through the window for good measure. He heard the sound of a man's body striking the ground, but he had no idea whether he had hit the man with the shot. His concern was for the baby. He had no way of knowing where the first man's errant shot had gone.

Hurriedly but with his gun ready, he turned up the lamp on the wall, bathing the room in yellow light. He looked down at the man on the floor, who was obviously dead.

He was worried because, in spite of all the noise, the baby was not crying. Fearing what he would see, he removed the blanket from the chair and pulled the chair away.

As he looked down at the baby she looked up at him and drooled. It was the most beautiful thing he had ever seen in his life.

SIXTEEN

Sheriff George Proctor looked down at the body in the doorway and stepped over it. His eyes swept the room, taking in the shattered glass on the floor, and then he looked at Clint Adams, who was seated on the bed holding the baby. The vision of the Gunsmith holding a baby seemed odd to him.

"Is the baby all right?" Proctor asked.

Strangely, Clint liked the man better for asking the question.

"She's fine," he said. "She didn't even cry."

Outside the room people were craning their necks, trying to look inside. Proctor had a deputy out in the hall, trying to push them back.

"Nothin' to see, nothin' to see," the deputy was saying. "Get on back to your rooms."

"I'll have you moved to another room," Proctor said.

"Appreciate it," Clint said. "What about the one at the window?"

"He hit the ground runnin', I think," Proctor said. "Did you get him?"

"Got him across the face with my gun barrel," Clint said. "I don't know if I winged him, though."

"May have a busted nose at the very least," Proctor said. "My men will be on the lookout for him."

"Who do you think sent them?" Clint asked the lawman.

Proctor frowned.

"What makes you think someone sent them?" he asked. "You do have a reputation, you know."

"Oh, come on, Sheriff . . ." Clint said, chiding the man.

"Who do *you* think sent them?" Proctor shot back.

"Vic Ward wants to keep me away from Loretta Kane real bad," Clint said.

"So bad he'd send someone to kill you?" Proctor asked. "I think not."

"Maybe they weren't going to kill me," Clint said. "Maybe they were just going to deliver a message. Either way, they put this baby's life in jeopardy. If I find out for certain that Ward was behind this—"

"Stop right there, Adams," Proctor said. "Don't go threatening the life of one of this town's leading citizens. Not in front of the law."

"I'm not threatening anyone, Sheriff," Clint said, looking down at the baby. "I'm making you a promise."

"Ah, Adams—"

"Sheriff?" the deputy said from the door. "I've got some men together to remove the body."

"Well, then, remove it."

"Uh, where do we take it, Sheriff?"

"Where would you take a dead body, Rafe?" Proctor asked impatiently.

"Uh, to the undertaker's, Sheriff."

"Very good, Rafe."

"Thanks, Sheriff."

"Rafe?"

"Yeah, Sheriff?"

"See if he's got anything in his pockets to tell us who he is."

"Sure, Sheriff," the man said, bending over.

"Not here!" Proctor barked. "Get it the hell out of here first."

"Yes, sir."

Three men stepped into the doorway, lifted the body, and carried it out of the room and down the hall.

"Rafe!" Proctor yelled.

"Yes, Sheriff?"

"Tell the desk clerk to give Mr. Adams a different room," Proctor said. "One without the low roof outside the window."

"Yes, Sheriff."

Proctor turned his attention back to Clint and the baby.

"You know," he said, "for the good of that baby I'd advise you to get her out of town."

"Are you *telling* me to get out of town, Sheriff?" Clint asked.

"No, I'm not, damn it," Proctor said, "I'm just giving you some friendly advice."

"I'll consider it."

"Yeah," Proctor said, "sure you will." He walked over to the window, looked outside, then turned to face Clint again.

"Look, I've got an idea."

"I'm listening."

Proctor looked at the open door. There were still some people milling about in the hall. He walked to the door and closed it.

"There's a rooming house down at the other end of town," Proctor said. "I'll get you a room there where you can leave the baby with someone." Proctor surprised Clint by bending over and looking at the baby. "I think she'll be safer if she's not in the same room with you."

Clint stared at the man and then said, "That's a fine idea, Sheriff. Do you think Mrs. Gordon will be able to stay with her?"

"I'm sure she can be convinced," Proctor said. "If not, there are other women in town. Maybe they can take turns."

"Much obliged for the help, Sheriff," Clint said. "I have to admit that you're something of a surprise to me tonight."

"Yeah," Proctor said. "Well, prepared to be surprised again."

"I don't know if I can handle all of this," Clint said, "but fire away."

"I also intend to get you together with Loretta, if I can."

That did surprise Clint.

"What changed your mind?"

"Vic Ward changed my mind," Proctor said. "I'm not convinced that Loretta herself didn't want to see you tonight."

"That's what I was thinking," Clint said. "I understand that he pretty much has her under his control."

"Where did you hear that?"

"Let's just say I've made one or two friends in town." He didn't want to mention Shannon's name. Not just yet. "Do you have any other reasons for being so helpful all of a sudden? Not that I'm looking a gift horse in the mouth, mind you."

"Also," Proctor said, "if Ward was responsible for this tonight, he's put me squarely on your side."

"Are you sure this little tyke didn't have something to do with it, too?"

Proctor extended his right index finger to the baby, who grabbed it and held it tightly.

"What do you think?" Proctor asked.

SEVENTEEN

Dan McGirt had taken a room behind the general store. The only entrance to the room was by the door in back. He preferred it that way, so the room was perfect for him.

When the knock came at the door, he looked quickly at Tina, who was asleep, then slid from the bed and answered the door naked, but for the gun in his hand.

It was Eddie Drake, one of the men he had sent after Clint Adams. All it took was one look at the man's bloody face and awkward posture for McGirt to know that they had failed.

"Did anyone see you?" he asked right away.

"I don't think so, Dan—Jesus, I think I got some busted ribs. I *know* my nose is busted."

"You're lucky that's all you got," McGirt said. "What happened to Gaines?"

"He's dead," Drake said. "Adams got him."

"What happened to Adams?"

"Nothin'."

"Great."

"It wasn't our fault, Dan," Drake said. "He musta knowed we was coming—"

"He didn't know you were coming," McGirt said. "You probably made too much noise."

"We was quiet, Dan," Drake said. "I swear."

"Yeah, you swear," McGirt said. "Wait here."

He went back into his room to his dresser and grabbed his wallet.

"Dan, honey?" Tina called from the bed. "Is something wrong?"

"Nothin', darlin'," McGirt said. "Go back to sleep. I'll be right there."

"Then I ain't goin' back to sleep," she said sleepily.

"That's even better," he said, going back to the door. "Here," he said, handing some money to Drake. "Get out of town."

"I need a doctor, Dan," Drake complained.

"Get one out of town," McGirt said. "I don't want the sheriff gettin' ahold of you."

"Gee, Dan—"

"Don't become a liability, Eddie," McGirt said to the man. "You know what happens to liabilities, don't you?"

Eddie Drake swallowed hard and said, "Sure, Dan, I know."

"Let me know where you are and I'll let you know when you can come back. All right?"

"Sure, Dan," Drake said. "Thanks for the extra money."

"Get out of here," McGirt said. "I don't want Tina to see you."

McGirt closed the door and went back to the bed. He slid in next to Tina, who was so warm her skin almost burned his. He turned toward her and saw that she was fast asleep. It was just as well. He had other things on his mind, anyway.

Shannon was roused from a deep sleep by the sound of the shots. She didn't know how many there had been, but she knew she had heard shots through the curtains of sleep. She got up from bed and walked to the window. Down the street she saw a group of men leaving the hotel, carrying something between them.

Hurriedly, she grabbed some clothes, threw them on, and ran out.

Through an alcoholic haze Victor Ward thought he heard shots. He lifted his head from his desk, where he'd been lying in a pool of brandy and saliva, and then lowered it again. In seconds, he was snoring.

Running into the lobby of the hotel, Shannon ran smack into Sheriff George Proctor.

"Whoa," he said, catching her as she bounced off of him, "what's the hurry?"

"I heard shots," she said. "Who'd they just carry out of here, Sheriff?"

He frowned and asked, "Who did you think they carried out, Shannon?"

"Well . . . I, uh, met a man earlier tonight. I thought it might be him."

"Would that man happen to be Clint Adams?"

"Yes," she said, "it would. Was it—"

"No, it wasn't him," Proctor said, releasing her,

"but it could have been. Two men broke into his room and there was gunfire."

"Is the baby all right?"

"You know about the baby?"

"Of course," she said. "Is she all right?"

"She's fine."

"Thank goodness."

"Shannon, what do you know about all of this?"

"I don't know anything, Sheriff," she said. "The shooting woke me up and I was worried—about the baby, that is."

"Yes," Proctor said, "about the baby."

"Can I go now?"

"Sure," he said, stepping aside. As she hurried to the steps he called, "Shannon?"

"Yes?" she asked, turning to look at him.

"They're in room four this time."

"Thanks, Sheriff."

Proctor watched the pretty, buxom redhead bound up the stairs and thought, a few friends, huh?

EIGHTEEN

Clint sat in the straight-backed wooden chair, his feet propped up on the windowsill, and watched Shannon sleeping on the bed with the baby. The redhead had insisted on staying so Clint could get some sleep, but after a couple of hours Clint had insisted they change places, and Shannon, after a full day's work, had agreed.

Shannon had told Clint that she had literally run into the sheriff on her way into the hotel. Clint hoped that word would not get back to Vic Ward about her helping him.

Clint wondered how much the sheriff really knew about Vic Ward. Clint had a couple of ways to find out for himself. He could send a telegram to Rick Hartman and have him find out for him. He could also wire San Francisco for the information. He knew a Chinese private detective there named Sam Wing, who could get it for him. In the end he decided to go right to the horse's mouth for what he wanted to know. He'd telegram Wing as soon as the telegraph office opened. He also wanted to wire Sheriff Tom Bush in Tyler Falls, to see if he had found out anything about the baby's mother, Sally Rise.

As first light filtered in through the window, Clint knew that the baby would be hungry when she woke up. He took the two baby bottles and went downstairs to the dining room to have them cleaned and filled with milk. When he returned he could hear the baby crying from the hall. As he entered, a harried-looking Shannon looked up from the bed, where she sat holding the baby. Her long red hair was flying all about, in disarray from sleeping. She was beautiful.

"You're beautiful in the morning," he said to her.

"Shut up, give me the damned bottle, and don't look at me."

"Grouchy, too, I see," he said, handing her one of the bottles.

Shannon took the bottle and pressed the nipple to the baby's mouth. The toothless gums and pink lips closed over it, and the baby started sucking greedily.

"You always this grouchy in the morning?" he asked her.

"Only when a man I like sees what a mess I am when I wake up. Why don't you go take a walk someplace?"

"There are one or two errands I can run," he said, "but when I get back you can go home and get dressed, and I'll buy you some breakfast."

"You've got a deal, friend," she said.

"There's only one problem."

"What's that?"

"You'll be seen with me, and word is bound to get back to Vic Ward."

"You forget," she said, "I don't belong to Victor Ward."

"You could get fired."

"That should be the worst thing that happens to me in my life," she said without concern. "Now go, already. I'm almost as hungry as this baby, and it's going to take a lot more than milk to satisfy me."

NINETEEN

As it turned out, there weren't very many errands he could run in Doyle that early. He decided to stop in at the livery, check on Duke, and pick up something from his rig.

The big gelding was doing okay, although he would have been happier out stretching his legs somewhere than cooped up in that stable.

His team, on the other hand, was somewhat lazier and seemed perfectly content to stand in their stalls.

The stock checked, he walked to the rig and climbed into the back. It took him a few minutes to find what he wanted, because he hadn't much use for it lately. It was the little New Line Colt he used as a belly gun when he needed something he could hide. He checked the action on the gun, and the loads and found it in working order, although it probably could have used a cleaning he didn't have time to give it. He unbuttoned his shirt, tucked the little .25-caliber gun into his belt, and then buttoned the shirt over it.

That done, he walked back to the hotel to give Shannon a chance to go home and change before they had breakfast.

In the hotel dining room a little while later it struck Clint that the three of them sitting there made a very domestic picture, Shannon eating with one hand and holding the baby in the other arm.

"You do that very well," he said, "very naturally."

"I was the oldest of eight brothers and sisters," she said, "so I had plenty of practice."

"Is that why you left?"

"What makes you think I left?"

"Didn't you?"

"Yes," she said, "but not because of my brothers and sisters. They were seven good reasons for me to stay, but I had one good reason to leave."

"And what was that?"

"It's an old story," she said. "My mother died, and my father wanted me to replace her in more ways than one."

"I see."

"Naturally," she said, "I always feel guilty when I talk about it."

"Why?"

"I wonder if he's not doing the same thing to one of my sisters right now," she said. "Two of them would be of age now, thirteen and fifteen."

"Is that when he started in with you?"

"I was an early bloomer," she said. "I had a woman's body when I was eleven, and he noticed. I left when I was fourteen. I put up with it for as long as I could for the sake of my brothers and sisters, but I finally had enough. I haven't seen any of them since I left ten years ago." She got a faraway look in her green eyes and said, "I miss them."

"Well, the experience hasn't seem to have, uh, affected you too badly."

"Oh, it was a long time before I could let a man touch me," she said, "and then I found out that I could get a lot of things I wanted just by spreading my legs. I went from one extreme to the other, and it took me even longer to find a happy medium. I think I'm pretty normal, now—as normal as I can be while working in a saloon as a whore."

"Saloon girl or whore?" he asked. "It's not necessarily the same thing."

"That's true," she said. "As long as the customers buy drinks, Vic doesn't make us sleep with them. That's up to us." She pressed her foot to his leg, running it up and down his shin, and said, "It's even up to us whether we charge money or not."

"Maybe I'll be one of the lucky ones."

"Maybe," she said, removing her foot.

When they finished breakfast, Clint asked Shannon what she would be doing with the rest of her day.

She smiled at him and said, "I have the feeling I'm going to be watching this precious little baby."

"If you would," he said, "but not here. On the sheriff's suggestion, we're going to move her. She'll be safer in another room."

"That's a good idea."

"Let's go over to the sheriff's office now. He's supposed to take us over to a rooming house at the other end of town."

"I know it," she said. "I stayed there when I first came to town. Not many people stay there, though."

"Good," he said, standing up. He hurried around the table to help her to her feet.

As they reached the lobby he stopped her and said, "Maybe you'd better let me carry the baby, and you go on ahead."

"Still think I'm afraid to be seen with you?" she asked.

"No, I know you're not afraid, but I am," he said. "Besides, this way you can continue to be my little secret weapon."

"Ooh, I like the way that sounds," she said. "All right, here."

Clint took the baby in his left arm, keeping the right hand free.

"Okay, go ahead," he told her. "I'll meet you at the rooming house."

"All right," she said. "Be careful."

He gave her a two-minute head start and then left the hotel and headed for the sheriff's office.

As Clint entered the sheriff's office, Proctor looked up from something he was reading.

"Morning, Sheriff."

"Mr. Adams."

"Sheriff," Clint said, "since you're almost on my side, I think you should call me Clint."

"All right, Clint."

"Did you arrange for that room at the rooming house?" Clint asked.

"Yes," Proctor said. He had a piece of paper that looked like a telegram in his hand. The paper was folded neatly in half. "I'll take you over there in a little while. Maybe you'd better read this first."

Proctor held the telegram out to Clint.

"Why don't you tell me what it says, Sheriff?"

"All right," Proctor said. "It's from Sheriff Bush, in Tyler Falls."

"About the baby's mother?"

"Yeah," Proctor said, dropping the telegram on the desktop. "They found her yesterday. She's dead."

TWENTY

They walked over to the rooming house in silence. As they approached it, Clint finally spoke.

"I guess Bush still doesn't know who hit the stagecoach."

"I guess not."

"Or how many people were taken off."

"If he knows," Proctor said, "he didn't put it in the telegram."

"Sheriff," Clint said, "how much do you know about Vic Ward?"

"What is there to know?" Proctor asked. "He came here from San Francisco, bought the saloon—which was a dump, by the way, when he bought it—and turned it into a going concern."

"Well, I know a detective in San Francisco. I'm going to wire him and asked him to check on Ward for me."

"I don't know why you're doing it," Proctor said,

"but I'd be very interested in what you find out."

"I'll let you know."

"Have you spoken to Mrs. Gordon yet about watching the baby?"

"Not yet," Clint said, "but Shannon should be waiting for us inside."

"You and Shannon have become very friendly pretty quick, haven't you?" Proctor asked.

"I guess you could say so," Clint said. "I've discovered that babies can bring that kind of thing out in people. Haven't you discovered that, Sheriff?"

Proctor scowled and said, "Yeah, I guess I have."

They went up to the front door of the rooming house and knocked. The door was opened by Shannon.

"Mrs. Muldoon is in the kitchen," Shannon said. "She's making her preserves. Since she doesn't rent out very many rooms, she makes a living by selling her preserves."

Clint and Proctor followed her inside, and Proctor closed the door.

"She said we can have any room in the house."

"Why don't you take the baby," Clint said to her. "I've got to send a telegram and talk to Mrs. Gordon. If she agrees, she'll come by later to spell you so you can get ready for work."

"All right," Shannon said, taking the baby. "What's wrong, Clint? You look—"

"We heard from the sheriff in Tyler Falls this morning," Clint said.

"The baby's mother?" she asked.

He nodded and said, "They found her dead."

"Oh, my God," Shannon said, hugging the baby. "That's awful. How?"

"That we don't know," Clint said, and then he looked at Proctor and said, "but now it's imperative that I talk to Loretta Kane."

Proctor nodded and said, "I'll set it up."

"I'll check back with you at your office later," Clint said.

"You poor thing," Shannon said to the baby.

"Where can I find Mrs. Gordon?"

Sheriff Proctor gave Clint directions to Mrs. Gordon's house.

"I'll talk to her after I send my telegram," Clint said. "Shannon, I'll see you later."

She nodded, still hugging the baby. Clint could see that there were tears in her eyes. Apparently he had found the proverbial whore with the heart of gold.

"I'll walk with you," Proctor said. "I think maybe I'll send Sheriff Bush a telegram asking for more information."

"That'd be helpful," Clint said.

"Not to this baby it won't," Shannon said. "Her mother's dead, and she don't much care how or why."

Clint pretty much agreed with her.

TWENTY-ONE

Clint stopped at the telegraph office and sent off a telegram to Sam Wing in San Francisco. After that he went over to Mrs. Gordon's house and spoke to her about watching the baby. When she asked him who was watching the baby now, he told her.

"A saloon girl?"

"She knows how to care for a baby, Mrs. Gordon. You and she could split the time, if you would."

Mrs. Gordon looked doubtful.

"I'll take care of that child, but I don't know about letting a saloon girl next to her."

"Talk to the saloon girl first and then form an opinion, Mrs. Gordon. That's all I ask."

"I suppose everybody deserves a chance," she said.

"Especially that baby."

"What about her?" Mrs. Gordon said. "They find her mother yet?"

"Yes," Clint said. "They found her yesterday. She was dead."

Mrs. Gordon's hands flew to her mouth.

"That poor child," she said. "I'll get over to the rooming house right away."

"And give Shannon a chance, Mrs. Gordon."

Mrs. Gordon whipped a shawl around her shoulders and looked at him.

"If she's giving that child some help," she said, "then I guess she deserves a chance."

They left the house together. Out on the porch she grabbed his arm. Her grip was surprisingly strong.

"Is that baby's kin in this town?"

"Yes," he said, "her mother's sister."

"Then she'll take the baby?"

"I don't know, Mrs. Gordon," Clint said. "I haven't talked to her yet."

"If she's that child's aunt," Mrs. Gordon said, "she's got to take her."

"I'm afraid not everybody thinks that way, Mrs. Gordon."

While Clint ran his errands, George Proctor went to see Vic Ward. When Ward let him in the saloon, it was clear from the way Ward looked that he had drunk himself to sleep last night and had probably never made it to bed. The man stunk from the kind of sweat you get from a drunk.

"I guess you heard about the excitement last night."

"What excitement?" Ward said, rubbing his hands over his face.

"A couple of men tried to kill Clint Adams last night," Proctor said.

"Is that a fact?"

"One of them is dead. The other one got away."

"Why are you telling me this?" Ward asked. "Do you think I had something to do with it?"

"If you did," Proctor said, "I'll get you for it, Ward."

"Yeah," Ward said, "you'll get me—you'll get me so I'll be out of the way and you can have a clear field with Loretta."

"Speaking of Loretta," Proctor said, "you're going to let her talk to Clint Adams today."

"I am, huh?"

"That's right," Proctor said.

"You tellin' me that as sheriff?"

"That's right," Proctor said. "There's a murder involved now, and Loretta is involved."

"How?"

"She'll tell you that after he and I tell her," Proctor said. "He and I will be back here at noon, and she'd better be here, Ward. If she's not, I'm gonna lock you up for obstructing justice. You understand?"

"Yeah," Ward said sourly, "I understand."

"And take a bath, for Chrissake," Proctor said. "You look like a wreck, and you stink."

"Get out of here!" Ward snapped.

"Noon," Proctor said, and left.

After the sheriff left, Ward went back to his office and poured himself a brandy. He thought hard back to last night. He remembered calling Dan McGirt into his office, but he didn't remember what they had talked about.

Had he told McGirt to have Adams killed? For the life of him, he just couldn't remember. He looked down at the brandy in his hand, then downed the drink.

He'd call McGirt in later and find out what happened, and he would do it without admitting that he couldn't remember. He poured one more brandy. He needed it. After that he would take a bath and get dressed, then talk to Loretta. She had to understand that he had to be present when she talked to Clint Adams. He wanted to know exactly what was going on.

There was absolutely no way Clint Adams was going to talk to her alone.

TWENTY-TWO

"I want to talk to her alone," Clint said.

Ward exploded.

"Absolutely not."

"Go ahead," Proctor said. "Go on up and talk to her alone."

"I forbid it!" Ward said, his face suffused with blood. He looked as if he were literally going to explode.

"Vic," Proctor said amiably, "if you try to stop him from going upstairs, I'll shoot you in the leg."

"You wouldn't dare," Ward said. "I'd have your job."

"You're obstructing," Proctor said, "and I'd be well within my rights as a lawman."

Ward glared at Proctor.

"Clint," Proctor said, "you go on up and talk to the lady. I'll keep Mr. Ward company down here. I know, Vic," he added to Ward, "we'll drink your beer while we wait."

"I hope you choke on it," Ward said.

Clint ignored them and went up the stairs to the second floor. He'd been told that Loretta Kane's room was the first one on the left. He walked to the door and knocked.

"Come on," a woman called.

Clint entered and closed the door behind him. Loretta Kane had her back to him.

"Miss Kane," he said, "I'm Clint Adams."

When she turned, he was surprised. Given the depth of feeling that both Proctor and Ward had for her, he had expected a raving beauty. She was certainly lovely, but she was not the heart-stopping beauty he had expected.

She had dark hair piled high on her head, and creamy skin. Her exposed throat was long and smooth, as were the slopes of her firm breasts. Her face was made up for work in the saloon, and he thought he detected a swelling on one cheek, beneath the makeup.

Her eyes were dark and set too widely apart, her nose was a little too long, and her mouth was too small. He suddenly realized that when you dissected her face into parts, they were all just a little too . . . off. However, when you put it all together, she was striking. The longer he stared at her, the less hard it became to believe that she could command the love of two men.

He guessed that she was in her late twenties. She was probably the older sister.

She appeared to be very nervous. She was constantly twisting and tugging at a handkerchief she held in her hand.

"Mr. Adams," she said, "I'm sorry I didn't answer

your telegram, but I thought Sheriff Proctor—"

"Miss Kane," he said, cutting her off, "they found your sister yesterday."

"Well . . . that's good news. . . ."

"No," he said, "it isn't. She's dead."

She stared at him for a few moments, until he thought perhaps she hadn't heard him. Then she said, "What?" and took one step forward. If he hadn't moved so fast she would have fallen. He caught her, her deadweight heavy in his arms. She hadn't fainted, but she had gone completely limp.

"Sally . . . dead?" she said.

"Here," he said, moving her to the bed, "sit down."

He left her on the bed and looked around the room for water. There was none, but there was a brandy decanter. He poured her a glass and gave it to her.

"I can't believe . . ." she said, then paused to sip the brandy. "How did it happen?" she asked, her voice stronger.

"We're not real clear on that, Miss Kane," Clint said. "I've been trying to talk to you since yesterday, but Vic Ward has been blocking me."

"I know," she said, "I wanted to—Vic said it would be better for me if I didn't."

"Better for you?" he asked. "Or for him?"

She looked up at him and handed him back the glass.

"I understand there was an attempt on your life last night."

"That's right."

"Is . . . is the baby all right?"

"She's fine," Clint said. "I need your help, Miss Kane."

"I can't . . . help myself," she said, fluttering her hands helplessly. "How could I help a small baby?"

"Well, for one thing," he said, "you could tell me her name."

Clint had expected that Loretta would need to look at an old letter for the name, but she surprised him.

"Her name is Katherine," she said, "Katherine . . . Loretta."

"Your sister named her after you?"

"After our mother and me."

"Loretta," Clint said. "I can understand if you don't want the baby—"

"It's not a question of wanting," she said, interrupting him. "I am not in any position to raise a child, whether I want her or not."

"Look," he said, "I don't know exactly what your problems are, but I'm sure the sheriff could help you with them. Hell, if there's anything I can do to help you, just let me know, but right now I need your help so I can do the right thing for that child . . . for Katherine."

She passed a hand across her forehead and eyes and asked, "What do you want me to do?"

TWENTY-THREE

"Since you don't want—I mean, since you can't take the baby, maybe you'll tell me who will?"

"How would I know?"

"I've got this letter that you sent to your sister, telling her not to come."

"That's how you found me."

"Yes." He handed her the letter.

"She should have listened to me."

"I guess she should have," Clint said, "but she didn't. What about this address? Is that where her husband's folks live?"

"Them?" Loretta said with disdain. "They never wanted their son to marry my sister."

"Well," Clint said, "they are blood kin to Katherine. If you can't take her, maybe they can."

"They wouldn't!"

"I guess you've helped me enough, Loretta," Clint said. He took the letter from her hand. "I'll need this for the address. Katherine and I will be leaving tomorrow to head back East."

He started for the door and she said, "No, wait!"

When he turned she was standing up, rubbing her palms on her dress, as if they were all sweaty.

"What, Loretta?"

"Um . . ." she said, licking her lips. "Give me a chance to think."

He studied her for a moment, then said, "All right, Loretta. I'll wait one more day. You let me know by tomorrow night what you want to do."

She patted her hair nervously with one hand and said, "Um, all right, all right."

He turned and walked back to her.

"Loretta, I meant what I said before. If you need any help, let me know."

He touched her cheek with his thumb and felt the swelling there.

"Nobody should have to put up with this."

"I fell."

"Yeah," he said, "I know." He walked to the door and said, "Remember what I said."

"I'll let you know by tomorrow night."

He turned in the open doorway and said, "I mean about the help. It'll be there whenever you need it, Loretta."

Downstairs, Proctor and Ward were still standing at the empty bar. Vic Ward was fidgeting impatiently, and when he saw Clint he turned and took several steps toward the stairs.

"Well?" Ward asked.

"Well what?" Clint asked.

Ward turned and look at Proctor, then back at Clint.

"What happened?"

"That'll be up to her to tell you," Clint said, coming down the rest of the way.

Ward started past him, and Clint grabbed his arm.

"Let go of my arm."

"Loretta and I will talk again tomorrow night, Ward," he said tightly. "Between now and then, if she comes up with one more bruise, you'll get it back . . . in spades. Do I make myself clear?"

"Sheriff," Ward said, "this man is threatening me. What are you gonna do about it?"

There was no answer.

"Sheriff?"

Ward turned and saw that Proctor was gone.

"Just remember what I said, Vic," Clint said. "I'll see you again. . . ."

He released Ward's arm and left the saloon. Vic Ward looked up the stairs, then turned and walked to his office.

Proctor was waiting for Clint outside.

"What happened?" he asked.

"I told her I was taking the baby back East, to her sister's in-laws."

"And?"

"And she asked me to give her a day."

"What does she expect to accomplish in a day?" Proctor asked.

"I don't know," Clint said, "but I offered her my help. She had a fresh swelling on her cheek."

"That bastard!" Proctor said.

"Come on, Sheriff," Clint said, "don't get all righteous now."

"What do you mean?"

"You must have known what was going on before this," Clint said, "and you've never done anything about it before."

"I—" Proctor started, but stopped.

"He's got some kind of a hold on her," Clint said, "and she's going to need help to break it."

"I'll help her," Proctor said. "I swear I will."

"I tell you what," Clint said, clapping the man on the shoulder. "Why don't we both help her?"

TWENTY-FOUR

Clint went back to Proctor's office with him.

"Coffee?"

"Why not?" Clint said.

Proctor poured two cups and handed Clint one. Proctor sat behind his desk, and Clint in front.

"What about that dead man?" Clint asked. "Can you tie him to Vic Ward?"

"No," Proctor said. "There was nothing on him even to give us his name, let alone tie him to Vic."

"I take it you didn't know the man?"

Proctor shook his head.

"He wasn't one of Vic's regular headbreakers."

"If he did work for Ward," Clint said, "who would he have taken his orders from?"

"That's easy," Proctor said. "McGirt."

"Who's McGirt?"

"Dan McGirt," Proctor said. "If Vic was a rancher, McGirt would be his ramrod. I guess that makes him his . . . right hand."

"Tell me about McGirt."

"Nothing much to tell," Proctor said. "He's young, about twenty-eight." Proctor frowned and said, "Come to think of it, all of Ward's men are under thirty. I think McGirt's the one who hired them."

"I guess he wanted young men," Clint said, "men who wouldn't be influenced."

"By what?"

"By anything," Clint said. He sat forward then and said, "Certainly not by my reputation."

"So you figure Ward had McGirt send those two men after you."

"That's what I figure," Clint said, sitting back. "Tell me: Have you checked with the doctor to see if the other man was treated?"

"I checked," Proctor said. "He hasn't treated anyone."

"What about surrounding towns?" Clint asked. "Have you checked with their doctors?"

"I hadn't thought of that," Proctor admitted. "I'll send out some telegrams."

Clint finished his coffee and set the empty cup down on the desk.

"What can we do for Loretta?" Proctor asked.

"Well," Clint said, "we could get her away from Vic Ward. Maybe then she'd be able to make up her own mind about what she wants to do."

"If I could get her away from Vic," Proctor said, "maybe I could get her to marry me."

"You feel that strongly about her?"

"I've asked her a dozen times to leave the saloon and marry me," Proctor said.

"Maybe she doesn't see herself as a lawman's wife," Clint suggested.

"Maybe."

"Or maybe Vic Ward just won't let her go," Clint added, rocking his chair back off its front legs. "How many men does he have?"

"About four, I guess," Proctor said. "They work the saloon in shifts."

"He's got four that he lets you see, you mean," Clint said.

"I suppose."

"If we can get Loretta away from him," Clint said, "maybe she could identify the dead man. Maybe she could give us the link we need."

"Maybe," Proctor said, "but I don't think we can just walk in there and walk out with her. Not with his men around."

"Well, then," Clint said, dropping the chair's front legs to the floor, "I guess we'll just have to think of a way around them. We've got until tomorrow night to think of a way."

"Tomorrow night?"

Clint nodded and stood up.

"That's when I'm supposed to talk to her next," Clint said. "She's going to tell me what to do with the baby."

"I wonder what she'll decide."

"I guess that depends on what *we* decide," Clint said. "You know, if you're not careful, you could come out of this with a wife and a baby, all at once."

Proctor didn't know what to say to that.

When Clint left the sheriff's office he went directly to the rooming house to check on the baby. Mrs. Gordon was there with her.

"Her name is Katherine," he told her. "Katherine Loretta Rise."

"Katherine," Mrs. Gordon said, trying it out. She looked down at the little bundle in her arms and said, "At last we have a name for you. Katherine . . . Katy." She looked at Clint and said, "I like Katy."

"Katy it is, then," Clint said. "So tell me, Mrs. Gordon, what did you think of Shannon?"

"A fine girl," Mrs. Gordon said. "What a fine girl like that is doing working in a saloon I'll never know."

"You'll have to take that up with her, I'm afraid, Mrs. Gordon."

"Do you know what she needs?" the woman asked.

"What does she need?"

"A nice young man to take her out of that place and marry her."

"Well," Clint said without a hitch, "that leaves me out, because I'm neither nice nor young."

"To me," Mrs. Gordon said, "you're young."

Clint smiled at her and said, "If I ever decide to get married, Mrs. Gordon, I'll come and see you."

"If my mister was still alive you wouldn't be talking like that."

"I surely wouldn't," Clint said. "I'm trying to find the baby a home, Mrs. Gordon. I'm not trying to find myself a wife."

"Ever?"

He thought briefly of Joanna Morgan, the only woman he had ever asked to marry him. She had ended up dead on the frozen grounds of Alaska.

"Ever," he said.

She frowned.

"Are you intent on a lonely life, Clint Adams?" she asked.

"Not intent, Mrs. Gordon," he said. "Just resigned to it. Can you stay a while longer?"

"With this pretty thing I'll stay as long as you like," she said. "I've got nowhere to go and nothing else to do."

"I appreciate it," Clint said. "I'll be back later."

"You go and do what you have to do to get this sweet child a home."

He smiled back at her and said, "I'm doing my best, Mrs. Gordon."

TWENTY-FIVE

When the bartender showed up for work to prepare the bar for opening, Ward told him to find Dan McGirt.

"But Mr. Ward, I got to get the bar ready—"

"You work for me?"

"Well, yes, sir, but—"

"If you want to keep working for me, you'll do as you're told."

"Yes, sir."

Ward sat in his office, waiting for McGirt and staring at the brandy bottle. He had sworn to himself that he would not drink as much brandy as he had yesterday.

He hadn't yet gone up to talk to Loretta. He didn't trust himself yet. If he went now he might hit her, and he remembered what Clint Adams had told him. He wondered what Loretta had given Adams to make him say that. Once Adams was taken care of, then he'd go and talk to Loretta, and she would see who was in charge.

There was a knock on the door and he said, "Come in, damn it."

Dan McGirt came in and closed the door behind him.

"You wanted to see me?"

"What the hell happened last night?" Ward demanded loudly.

"Things didn't go the way I planned them, Mr. Ward," McGirt said. "But don't worry, I'm right on top of the situation."

"Is that a fact?"

"Well, sir, according to your own schedule, I still have several hours to get the job done."

"What happened to the men you sent last night?"

"One is dead," McGirt answered, "and I sent the other one out of town."

"Is there anything to connect them to you or me?" Ward asked.

"No, sir," McGirt said, "I was real careful about that. I didn't use any of the men we use in the saloon."

"All right," Ward said, hardly mollified. He still didn't know if he had told McGirt to kill Clint Adams or not, but he was about to make that abundantly clear, and he was sober enough to remember it.

"I want this very clear, McGirt," he said. "I don't want Adams to be walking around tomorrow. Do you know what I mean?"

McGirt didn't know why Ward didn't just come right out and say what he wanted.

"I understand, Mr. Ward," he said, "but let's make

it real clear, so there's no mistake later. Do you want me to kill him?"

"That's right," Ward said, "I want you to kill him."

McGirt nodded and said, "Done."

Upstairs Loretta Kane was standing at her window, rubbing her hands together over and over again. The only way she was going to be able to help Sally's daughter was to get away from Vic Ward. There was a time when she thought she loved Ward and would do anything he asked. Later it got to the point where she didn't love him but still would do what he told her. Now she was just flat-out afraid of the man. The one man she thought could help her was George Proctor, but Ward had sworn that if she went off with Proctor, he would have his men kill the sheriff.

Now, however, with the appearance of Clint Adams, maybe she finally had a way out. After all, he *was* the Gunsmith, and he did offer her his help.

She had been waiting for Vic Ward to come up and ask her what Adams wanted. That he hadn't yet led her to believe he was angry, and that that anger was building the longer he stayed away.

She knew that when Ward did come up, he would beat her. She wished now that she and Adams hadn't agreed to meet again tonight. She wanted to talk to him soon. There had to be a way to get a message out to him, if she could only think of it.

TWENTY-SIX

Clint went back to his hotel to check if a reply had come from San Francisco. The hotel was closer than the telegraph office, and he had left instructions that the reply should be taken to the hotel. This was one telegram the contents of which he wanted to see firsthand.

The clerk informed him there was no reply yet but that he had a guest.

"A guest?" Clint asked.

"Yes, sir," the clerk said. The man looked unsure of himself. "Well, sir, she said you were expecting her. Uh, weren't you expecting her?"

There was only one person it could be, and in a way, he *was* expecting.

"Oh, yes," he said to the clerk, "I'm expecting her, all right. Thanks."

He went upstairs to his room and used the key to open the door. Shannon was in his bed, with the sheet pulled up to her neck. Her nipples pressed out against the sheet, making it abundantly clear what she was wearing underneath it: nothing.

"You've made friends with Mrs. Gordon, I see," Clint said.

"And now," she said, dramatically, "I want to make friends with you."

"Well," he said, "I believe that can be arranged."

He unbuckled his gunbelt, removed his shirt, and went to sit by her on the bed. She grasped the edge of the sheet to remove it, but he grabbed her wrist and stopped her.

"I'll do it," he said.

But first he ran his hand over her body through the sheet. He started at her ankles and moved his hand upward. She had fine, strong calves and thighs. He could feel the tangle of hair beneath the sheet, but kept his hand moving over her flat belly. He was surprised that he could feel her ribs so clearly. When he put his hand on her breasts, he couldn't understand how a girl so otherwise slender could have such big breasts.

Slowly, he took the sheet in his hand and peeled it down, uncovering her breasts, her belly, and finally tossing the sheet off completely.

Throughout the whole thing she had her eyes closed, and now she opened them, breathing heavily.

"God," she said, her eyes shining, "you've got me so—so—"

"Ready," he said.

"Yes."

He put his hands on her breasts now, rubbing his palms over the burgeoning nipples. Her nipples were an odd pale color, as was the little circle around each. He bent over them one at a time, touching his tongue to them, then rolling them between his lips and finally nibbling them with his teeth. She lifted her hands to his head, but he in turn took her wrists in his hands and pinned her hands back to her sides.

"What are you doing to me?" she asked.

"Just lie still."

He continued to kiss her breasts, running his tongue down between them, tracing a wet path down to her navel and beyond. He kissed her belly and paused over the fragrant patch between her legs, inhaling the scent of her readiness. He continued on, kissing her thighs on the outside, biting the tender skin on the inside, and moved farther still. He kissed her calves, raising first one foot and then the other, rubbing them, kissing them, licking and sucking her toes.

"Jesus, God," she said, "nobody's ever kissed my feet. . . ."

"I want to taste every inch of you," he said.

He worked his way back up the other leg until he was back at the triangle of red hair between her legs. He kissed it gently, then probed with his lips until he could taste the tartness of her. She wiggled her hips and moaned as he licked the length of her moist slit, and then he delved inside of her and she gasped. Finally, when he centered on her stiff little clit, she moaned aloud and reached down to cup his head. This time he allowed her to use her hands. He sucked the little nub into his mouth, lashed it with his tongue, and then pursed his lips and sucked at it. She began to thrash about on the bed beneath him, and he felt her belly beginning to tremble as the release was building up inside her.

When she lifted her hips and cried out, he quickly abandoned his oral ministrations, mounted her, and drove himself home. She immediately wrapped her arms and legs around him. Her hands cupped his buttocks, and she tried to pull him even deeper inside her. She soared, and just as she was coming down, soared again. She grunted with the effort of trying to keep up with him as he pounded into her, seeking his own release. She closed her eyes tightly, and just when she thought it couldn't possibly get any better, he exploded inside her, and she stifled a scream by biting him on the shoulder. . . .

A little later she rolled over, one breast pressing warmly against him.

"You don't do this for a living, do you?" she asked him.

"No, ma'am," he said, "purely for pleasure."

"Um," she said, "you're very good at it, you know. I know what I'm talking about. No man has ever— I mean, you like to turned me inside out."

"I take it this is all your way of saying you enjoyed it?"

"Oh, yes," she said, kissing his chest, "oh, yes. . . ."

She kissed his chest, licking his nipples while pressing her breasts against him. Her head began to go lower, as her tongue moved wetly over him. Finally she was nestled between his legs and began to lick the length of his cock, holding his balls in her hand gently. When he was as stiff as he was going to get, she swooped down on him with her mouth, taking him in and sucking him deeply and wetly. He never would have thought that she could finish him so quickly, not after what they had just been through, but in a moment she had his hips and buttocks straining up off the bed as he exploded into her mouth. . . .

"Now, you *do* do this for a living," he said.

"Not this time, though, honey," she assured him.

She was lying on top of him, her cheek pressed to his chest. She lifted her head, kissed his neck, and then lowered her head again.

"This was for you and me," she said.

He put his arms around her and held her.

Sleepily she said, "I thought I'd never get you away from that little vixen."

TWENTY-SEVEN

They napped, and then he told her what he had found out from Loretta.

"Katherine," Shannon repeated. "I like that."

"Mrs. Gordon wants to call her Katy."

"I like that, too," she said. "What will you do now?"

"Well," Clint said, "I'd like to get Loretta away from Vic Ward, so she can speak her mind."

"How are you going to do that?" she asked. "He's always got men in the saloon."

"I know," Clint said. "We'll have to do it from the outside."

"Outside?" Shannon said. "Well, how are you going to get word to her about what you want to do?"

"I don't know," he said, running his hands down over her ass, kneading it with both hands. "I thought you might be able to help me with that."

She lifted her head and looked at him, her eyes dancing.

"Oh, sir," she said, "methinks you want to have your way with me in more ways than one."

"Methinks you are right, lass," he said.

They left the hotel together and walked toward the saloon.

"What if she won't talk to me?" Shannon asked.

"Use the magic words."

"And what are they?"

He smiled and said, "Clint Adams."

She laughed and said, "They're magic to me."

Loretta Kane was still looking out her window at the street below when she saw Clint Adams and Shannon walking together down the street toward the saloon. They stopped across the street, and they looked very friendly.

Maybe she could get a message to Clint Adams through Shannon. Loretta had never been very friendly with the other girls, and she didn't think that she and Shannon had ever said more than hello to each other.

What if Shannon wouldn't talk to her?

Tina Blake was also looking out her window at that moment, as she and Loretta had the rooms overlooking the street. Tina and Shannon were best friends, and Tina knew that Shannon was interested in the stranger. It was Shannon who told her that his name was Clint Adams and that he was a legendary gunman.

From her vantage point Tina could see the smile

on her friend's face. Shannon looked really happy. Tina knew all about Shannon's past and also knew that her friend had not had much happiness in her life. She was glad to see that smile on Shannon's face.

If the man was who she said he was, though, he would probably be moving on soon. That's the way men like him were. Tina had known plenty of men like that.

She hoped Shannon knew that as well.

Tina went back to her mirror, to finish making up her face and doing her hair. She wanted to look real pretty for Dan McGirt tonight.

Now, at least she had a man who was putting down roots here in Doyle. Dan had a real good job, and was being paid real well by Mr. Ward.

Shannon should get herself a man like Dan McGirt.

TWENTY-EIGHT

Loretta moved to her door and listened intently. Shannon's room was right down the hall, and the red-haired girl should be going there now to get ready for work. When Loretta heard the footsteps outside her door, she opened it, hoping she wasn't making a mistake.

She was surprised to see Shannon standing there, her hand raised to knock.

"Shannon."

"Hello, Loretta," Shannon said. "Were you expecting me?"

"I saw you outside, with Clint Adams," Loretta said. "Come in."

Shannon entered, and Loretta closed the door behind them.

"Why were you going to knock?" Loretta asked.

"I wanted to talk to you."

"And I wanted to talk to you."

"Well," Shannon said, "that's quite a switch from the past couple of years, isn't it?"

"Yes, it is," Loretta said. She wrung her hands nervously and said, "I know you have no reason to help me, Shannon—"

"Maybe not," Shannon said, "but I've got reason to help that baby."

"You—you know about the baby?"

"I've been taking care of her part of the time," Shannon said.

Suddenly Loretta smiled. It was a smile Shannon had never seen before. She had often thought that she and Loretta had something in common. Neither of them had ever smiled a real smile.

"What does she look like?"

Shannon smiled now.

"She's beautiful," Shannon said. "She's the most beautiful thing I've ever seen."

"Sally was like that," Loretta said. "My sister was the pretty one, Shannon. I mean, she was *really* and truly the pretty one."

Shannon stepped forward and put her hand on Loretta's arm.

"I'm sorry about your sister, Loretta."

Loretta looked at Shannon and said, "You know something? I haven't even cried yet. I haven't cried for my sister."

"Then cry, girl," Shannon said. "Go ahead and cry for her and for yourself."

Suddenly Loretta was in Shannon's arms, crying her heart out, and Shannon felt closer to this woman than she had felt to anyone in a long time. They had misery in common.

• • •

Clint walked to the telegraph office to check on a reply.

"Just came in," the clerk said. "I was gonna run it over to your hotel."

"I'll take it," Clint said. "Thanks."

Clint read the telegram from Sam Wing, then folded it and put it away. He wasn't sure yet if he wanted to show it to Sheriff Proctor. Right now Proctor was helping him in a more or less unofficial capacity. They were joining together to help Loretta, and that was a very personal thing for the lawman. If he showed him this telegram, then he'd have to act in his official capacity.

Clint wanted to keep Proctor unofficial for just a little while longer.

Tina was coming out of her room when she saw Shannon coming out of Loretta's. For some reason Tina ducked back into her room, not wanting Shannon to see her. When Shannon had something she wanted to talk about, she usually went to Tina. Why was she coming out of that uppity bitch Loretta's room?

For the first time in years, Loretta felt something other than despair. She also felt that she might just have something she hadn't had in a very long time: a friend.

Shannon entered her room shaking her head. She now knew something she had never known before. She knew that Loretta wasn't uppity as much as she was miserable. In her misery, she had pushed herself away from everyone. Shannon told Loretta that she used to do that, too, until she decided that the best way to handle misery was *not* to let anyone see it. Shannon felt ashamed of herself for having disliked Loretta for so long and for not recognizing her behavior for what it was.

Shannon now felt more than ever that she had to help Clint get Katherine together with her Aunt Loretta. They couldn't let Vic Ward and all the men he could find get in their way. Shannon had told Loretta everything Clint had told her, and made sure Loretta understood *what* they were going to do, what the consequences could be, and what the rewards probably would be. Loretta had been willing to go along with all of it.

Now all Shannon had to do was let Clint know.

TWENTY-NINE

When Tina saw Shannon enter her room, she left hers and went downstairs. She saw that Stacy was downstairs already, and went to tell the other girl what she saw.

"What do you suppose that's all about?" Stacy asked Tina.

"I don't know," Tina said. "Boy, you sure can't tell about some people. I thought the last person Shannon would ever want to talk to would be Loretta."

"What are you two gabbing about?" Dan McGirt asked from behind them.

Both women turned to look at him. Tina smiled widely, glad to see her man. Stacy, a tall, voluptuous brunette, knew that Tina would never understand if she found out that McGirt was sleeping with both of them. Stacy didn't mind sharing McGirt because he made her happy. Tina, however, would never share a man with anyone—willingly, that is.

From behind Tina, Stacy winked and smiled at Dan McGirt.

"We were talking about what I just saw," Tina said. "You won't believe it. . . ."

McGirt listened so intently that Tina even went further with her story and told McGirt how Shannon was probably sleeping with that gunfighter who was in town.

"And what gunfighter is that?" McGirt asked.

"Why, Clint Adams, of course," she said. "What other gunfighter is there in town? I mean, they call him the Gunsmith, don't they? Ain't he some kinda legend? That's what Shannon said, anyway—"

McGirt grabbed Tina by the shoulders and said, "Honey, wait, take a breath. Stacy, the bartender wants you."

Stacy turned and looked at the bartender, who was looking the other way.

"No, he don't—"

"Yes," McGirt said, "he does."

He gave her a meaningful look, which she understood right away. Stacy was a lot smarter than Tina was, which was why he had chosen to tell Stacy about Tina, but not Tina about Stacy. He wouldn't have been able to fool Stacy for this long.

"Now, Tina," McGirt said, "I want to go through all of this with you again, but more slowly this time. Tell me what you know, and tell me what you saw. Okay?"

"Well, sure, honey," Tina said.

He waited, then took a deep, calming breath and said, "All right, Tina: Start."

• • •

Clint was over at the sheriff's office, telling him what he had told Shannon.

"You really think that taking her out a window is gonna work?" Proctor asked.

"We can't go inside and take her," Clint said. "Ward has the inside covered."

"Yeah, but I'm the law," Proctor said.

Clint thought about the telegram in his pocket.

"I don't think that's going to matter much to Victor Ward, Sheriff," Clint said. "If we go in there and try to take Loretta out, there's going to be shooting. In a place as crowded and popular as the Bull's-eye, somebody is going to get hurt."

Proctor thought for a few moments and then said, "We're going to need a ladder."

After McGirt finished with Tina he went to Ward's office and told Ward what he thought was going to happen.

"They're gonna try to take her out."

"They can't," Ward said. "Double the men in the saloon."

"Mr. Ward," McGirt said, "I don't think they'll try it from inside."

"Why not? You think Adams is afraid to face a few guns?"

"No, I don't think he's afraid," McGirt said, "but he knows if he tries to take her out there's gonna be shooting. He and the sheriff won't want any innocent bystanders getting hurt."

"Then how?"

"From the outside."

"Outside?"

McGirt nodded.

"A window."

"That's crazy."

"Not so crazy," McGirt said. "All they need is a ladder. I think Clint sent Shannon to talk to Loretta, and to tell her to be ready."

"That bitch!" Ward said. His eyes went to the brandy decanter on his desk.

McGirt assumed that Ward meant Shannon. There was something both Tina and Stacy didn't know: Shannon was McGirt's first choice as a bedmate, but she had turned him down. McGirt thought that if she hadn't, he never would have bothered with the other two. Maybe now he'd have a chance to sample her Irish charms.

"I want her ass out of here!" Ward said. "Fire her. No, kill her."

"I think we should leave her right where she is . . . for a while, anyway."

"Why?"

"If we do something now, Adams will know that *we* know what he's up to."

Ward frowned and said, "You're right. We'll take care of her later."

"If you'll allow me to make a suggestion . . ." McGirt said.

"Go on."

"Let's double the men in the saloon, as you suggested. That'll make Adams think that we're covering the inside, and not the outside. Meanwhile, I'll put some men on the outside, covering the alley."

"All right," Ward said. "It's a good idea. Go ahead with it."

"Now there's another question," McGirt said.

"What?" Ward asked impatiently.

"I know you want Adams dead," McGirt said, "but Proctor is the law."

"He *was* the law," Ward said, eyeing the brandy decanter. He grabbed up a glass and poured it full, then downed it.

"Kill him, too," he said.

THIRTY

Since Clint and Proctor had to wait until dark before they could put their plan into effect, they went about their business until then. Sheriff Proctor went to the telegraph office to check on replies from doctors in other towns in the surrounding area. Clint went to the Bull's-eye just to make eye contact with Shannon. That's all he'd need for her to tell him that Loretta was ready to go along with the plan.

As he entered the Bull's-eye Saloon he saw that, already, even though it was early, they had doubled their men. There was now a man with a rifle in each of the four corners of the room.

Clint wondered if one of them was Dan McGirt. He decided to find out.

He walked to the bar and ordered a beer. As he turned to face the room, beer in hand, he spotted Shannon across the room. She gave him an almost imperceptible nod, which he did not return.

He turned to the bar again and called the bartender over.

"Yes, sir?"

"Is Dan McGirt here?"

"Dan?" he asked. "Uh, yeah, he's here."

"Which one is he?"

"He's in that far corner," the bartender said, using his chin to point. "Dressed all in black."

Clint used the mirror to look at the man dressed in black. Why didn't that surprise him?

He took his beer and walked toward that corner. McGirt had been lounging against the wall, and seeing Clint approach, straightened up.

"McGirt, right?"

"That's right," McGirt said. "Do I know you?"

"I think so," Clint said. "If you don't, you're probably going to get fired soon."

McGirt studied Clint for a few moments, then said, "Clint Adams, right?"

"Lucky guess?" Clint asked.

"What do you want, Mr. Adams?" McGirt asked. "I'm working."

"I just thought we should talk."

"Why?"

"Well . . . you did send a couple of men to kill me last night, didn't you?"

"What?" McGirt asked. "Are you crazy?"

"Well, anyway," Clint went on, "since your boss and I seem to be headed for a collision, I just thought it would be good if we met."

"What kind of a collision?"

"The kind he hires you for, son," Clint said.

McGirt's jaw tightened.

"Don't call me 'son.' "

"Well," Clint said, "you are a little younger than I am."

"A *lot* younger than you," McGirt said, sneering.

"Let's not go that far," Clint said.

"I know about your reputation, Adams," McGirt said. "I know they call you the Gunsmith, but all of that was a long time ago."

Clint feigned a frown and said, "It wasn't all that long ago."

"I just don't want you to think your reputation scares me."

"Oh, I knew that."

"You did?" McGirt looked confused.

"Oh, sure," Clint said. "Anybody who dresses all in black is sure to be tough, isn't that right? Tell me: Did you see somebody dress like this once? Maybe a gunman when you were little?"

"What are you talking about?" McGirt asked. "Are you making fun of the way I dress?"

"As a matter of fact," Clint said, "yes."

McGirt glared at Clint and said, "I should take you outside in the street, Adams."

"Why? Because I made fun of your clothes? I know I'm older than you are, but is that what your generation calls a reason to kill someone?"

McGirt opened his mouth to reply when he suddenly realized what Clint was doing.

"You're goading me."

"Smart boy."

"You want me to fight you."

"No."

"Sure you do."

"But you only fight for money, right?"

"Can you think of a better reason?"

"Lots," Clint said. "I've never sold my gun for money."

"Oh, yeah?" McGirt said. "Then how did you get that big rep?"

"What big rep?" Clint asked. "I thought you weren't impressed by big reps."

"I'm not."

"Let me give you some advice."

"Save it," McGirt said. "I don't need any advice from you."

"I think you do," Clint said, "so I'm going to give it to you."

"Well, then, give it and be on your way."

"In the future, when you sell your gun," Clint said, "make sure you sell it to the winning side—that is, if there *is* a future."

THIRTY-ONE

When Clint turned to leave the saloon, he saw George Proctor standing just inside the door.

"What was that all about?" the lawman asked.

"Just making his acquaintance."

"How did it go?"

"He's not as cool under fire as he thinks he is," Clint said. "Plus, he dresses funny. What are you doing here?"

"I got some replies from those other doctors," Proctor said as they left the saloon together.

"And?"

"A doctor in Garnett treated a man for a broken nose and bruised ribs."

"Where's Garnett?"

"Half a day's ride."

"Is he still there?"

"Yes," Proctor said. "I sent a telegram to the sheriff to hold him."

"You going over there?"

"I'm sending Rafe, my first deputy."

"Rafe? The one from the hotel shooting?"

"Yeah."

"He's your *first* deputy?"

Proctor sighed and said, "Yeah. He'll bring him back tomorrow."

"Hopefully," Clint said, "this will all be wrapped up by tomorrow."

"You know," Proctor said, "Vic might just let her go."

"If he did, that would work for you," Clint said. "It might even work for both of us. She'd be away from him, and maybe she would take the baby, and there wouldn't be any violence. But do you really think he'll let her leave?"

Proctor was quiet for a moment, then said, "No, I don't think he would."

"Do we have a ladder?"

"Yeah," Proctor said, "from the livery."

"What about your other deputies?" Clint said. "You going to get them in on this?"

"Hell, no," Proctor said. "This is unofficial. Besides, Rafe's my first deputy, remember?"

"I understand," Clint said. If Rafe was the first deputy, how smart could the others be?

"How about Loretta?" Proctor asked. "Does she understand what we're gonna do?"

"According to Shannon she does, yes."

They reached Proctor's office and stopped.

"Did you get a reply from your telegram to San Francisco yet?" Proctor asked.

"No," Clint lied. He hoped that Proctor didn't pick up on his split second of hesitation. If he showed

Proctor the telegram now, Proctor would have to arrest Ward, and Ward wouldn't come easily. Clint still felt he was right in waiting until they had Loretta free of Ward before showing Proctor the telegram.

"Well, let me know when you do."

"Sure," Clint said. "I'll meet you back here just before dark."

"Right."

Proctor went inside, and Clint went to the rooming house to give Mrs. Gordon a rest.

"The baby is sleeping upstairs," Mrs. Gordon said. "Mrs. Muldoon said that she'll help."

Mrs. Muldoon was white-haired, like Mrs. Gordon, but rail-thin, whereas Mrs. Gordon was more on the hefty side.

"She's such a sweet child," Mrs. Muldoon said, "and all I have to do is make my preserves."

"So you see," Mrs. Gordon said, "we don't need you."

"Well, then," Clint said, "what do you suggest I do?"

"Are you still looking for a home for Katy?"

"Of course," Clint said, "but I've got a couple of hours free."

"Well, don't spend it drinking," Mrs. Gordon said. "Go and get some rest."

"You know," Clint said, "that's not a bad idea."

THIRTY-TWO

After a couple of more brandies Victor Ward finally decided to go up and talk to Loretta Kane. It was time for him to find out what was going on. It was also time for him to remind her who was in charge.

He left his office, and as he entered the saloon he saw Clint Adams and Sheriff Proctor leaving.

"What did they want?" he asked McGirt.

"Adams wanted to introduce himself to me."

"And?"

"And we talked."

"About what?"

"About being on the winning side."

"You *are* on the winning side."

"That doesn't concern me," McGirt said. "I'm happy as long as I'm on the side of the money."

Ward frowned at McGirt.

"You mean you don't think you're on the winning side, McGirt?"

"Mr. Ward," McGirt said, "as long as you pay me, I'm on your side. I told you, whether it's the winning side or not doesn't matter to me. When this job is over, I'll go on to the next one. You see, I don't have any money, Mr. Ward, like you do, so I go where the money is."

"Well," Ward said, "the money is here, so you stay put."

"I'll stay put, Mr. Ward," McGirt said. "I won't have to move from here, because Adams will be coming to us."

"Yes," Ward said, "yes . . . I'm going upstairs. I'll be down in a . . . little while."

Ward went up the stairs, walked to Loretta's door, and knocked.

"Come in."

Ward opened the door and entered. Loretta stood up from her dressing table and faced him nervously.

"Vic."

"What did Clint Adams want?"

"He wanted to tell me that my . . . my sister is dead."

"How?"

"They—they're not sure," she said. "All I know is that she's dead."

"And that's all he wanted to tell you?" he demanded. "Don't lie to me, Loretta!"

"I won't lie," she said. Why was she so afraid of this man? "He brought my sister's baby with him."

"I know that."

"The baby needs a home, Vic."

"And he wants you to take her?"

"Or tell him who will," she said. "My sister's husband has family back East."

"So tell him to send the baby there."

"They won't take the baby, Vic," she said. "His family hated my sister."

"So? What's that to do with you?"

"That baby is my blood."

"So you're going to take her, and raise her here in a saloon?" he asked. He took two quick steps and gripped her arms tightly. She flinched, thinking he was going to hit her.

"Or do you intend to leave here with the baby? Is that it? You're going to leave here, leave me, after all I've done for you?"

"I'm not leaving, Vic," she said, "really."

"Loretta," he said, "if you tried to leave me you know what I would do to you."

"I told you—"

"I'd kill you."

"I'm not leaving, I said."

"You can bet you're not leaving me," Ward said, "because you're not leaving this building. Let's go."

"Go?" she asked. "Where?"

"You're staying downstairs, in my room."

"Your room?" Loretta asked. Inadvertently her eyes went to the window, which was to be her avenue of escape. "But why?"

"Because it has a lock," he said, "and I'm locking you in."

"But Vic—"

"Let's go," he said, dragging her to the door.

When Ward appeared on the steps, pulling Loretta after him, everyone looked. The saloon was not crowded, but there were still a good twenty people witnessing it, including Shannon.

She watched as Ward dragged Loretta through the saloon and through the curtained doorway. Shannon knew that hall led to Ward's office and his room. She also knew there were no windows back there.

Somehow she had to get to Clint and tell him his plan had just been ruined.

As Ward went past McGirt with Loretta in tow, the man in black said, "What are you doing?"

Ward pointed a finger at McGirt and said, "This is none of your business."

McGirt saw the look in Ward's bloodshot eyes and knew that the man was not only drunk, he was also crazy.

THIRTY-THREE

Shannon grabbed Tina by the arm and said, "I've got to go somewhere."

"What?" Tina asked. She'd been watching the action along with everyone else. "Where are you going?"

"Just cover for me," Shannon said.

"Shannon," Tina said, "what's going on with you and Loretta?"

"What are you talking about?"

Tina put her hands on her hips and said, "Now come on, honey, I saw you coming out of her room. Are you looking for a new best friend?"

"Wha—" Shannon said. "Tina . . . did you tell McGirt that you saw me?"

"Well . . . not exactly."

"What do you mean, 'not exactly'?"

"Well, I was telling Stacy, and Dan overheard, so then I had to tell him."

"Oh, Tina . . ."

"Well, I thought maybe you were looking for a new best friend!" Tina said, pouting.

"Tina," Shannon said, "you are so dumb!"

"I know that," Tina said, "but are we still friends?"

"Yes, Tina," Shannon said patiently, "we're still friends. I have to go out for a few minutes. Cover for me."

"When will you be back?"

"I'll be back before we get busy."

"But—but—what's going on?" Shannon heard Tina ask as she went out the batwing doors.

Clint had taken Mrs. Gordon's advice. He had gone back to his hotel room to lie down for a while. It wasn't even to sleep, it was just to have a moment alone—his first since he had found the baby. When the knock came at his door he thought, well, that didn't last long.

When he opened the door, Shannon darted in.

"It's all messed up," she said.

"What's all messed up?"

"Your plan," she said. "It's ruined."

"How?"

"Vic just dragged Loretta out of her room," Shannon explained. "I think he's going to lock her either in his room or his office."

"Are there any windows in those rooms?"

"No."

"That's great," he said, shaking his head. From the chair he grabbed his gunbelt and put it on. "I have to go and talk to the sheriff. You'd better get back to work before you're missed."

As they were going down the stairs he asked,

"What do you think happened?"

"I know what happened," she said, and told him about Tina seeing her coming out of Loretta's room.

"And she told McGirt," she finished.

"Wait a minute," he said, putting his hand on her arm to stop her before they stepped out of the hotel. "Does she know about me?"

"Well, sure," she said, "I told you that the first night."

"I mean, does she know about you and me?"

"Sure."

"Then she could have told McGirt that, too," he said, "and McGirt probably told Ward."

"So?"

"So that means Ward probably knows you're helping me," Clint said. "I don't think you should go back there."

"If I don't go back they're really going to think something's wrong," she said. "Don't worry about me. I'll be fine. You go and talk to the sheriff."

"Shannon—"

She silenced him with a quick but firm kiss on the mouth and said, "Go and do what you have to do. I'll be fine."

She darted out of the hotel before he could stop her, and he didn't want to chase her down the street. That would attract too much attention. He was going to have to take her at her word that she'd be all right.

He left the hotel and walked over to the sheriff's office.

"What do we do now?" Proctor asked after Clint had given him the news.

"Come up with a new plan," Clint said. "Ward knows that I'm supposed to talk to Loretta tonight."

"And you really think he's going to let you?"

"Well, if you come in an official capacity, he'll have to."

"If he doesn't want to break the law, yes," Proctor said. "What if he's beyond that?"

"Then he'd have to sic his men on us," Clint said. "How many of them want to shoot an officer of the law?"

"I don't know," Proctor said. "But how many does it take?"

"Yeah, you're right," Clint said. "Just one—and McGirt might be the type to give it a try."

"I'll make some coffee," Proctor said.

"We're gonna have to figure something out tonight," Clint said.

"Why tonight?" Proctor asked. "When Rafe brings that man back from Garnett, he'll probably tell you that he came after you because McGirt told him to, and McGirt works for Ward. That'll be enough for me to lock both of them up."

Clint took a deep breath and fished the telegram out of his pocket.

"If all you're looking for is a reason to arrest Ward, I've got a humdinger right here."

"What's that?"

"It's the telegram from San Francisco."

"When did you get this?"

"Earlier today."

"And you didn't tell me?"

"Read it, and then we'll argue."

Proctor read the thing, his eyes widening, and then he looked at Clint accusingly.

"This telegram says that Ward is wanted for questioning in San Francisco regarding the death of a policeman. You didn't think you should show me this?"

"No."

"Why not?"

"Let me explain."

"I can't wait," Proctor said, sitting behind his desk. "I'm all ears."

THIRTY-FOUR

Clint tried his best to explain his thinking to Proctor.

"Tell me," he said when he was finished, "what you intend to do now."

"I intend to arrest Victor Ward."

"See?" Clint said. "See what I mean? You're just going to walk in there and arrest him?"

"That's my job," Proctor said. "It's official now, Clint. I can even use my deputies."

"Somebody is still going to get killed," Clint said, "and remember, your first deputy is not here. You'd have to do this with your other deputies and me."

"You?" Proctor said. "You're not even involved anymore."

"What are you talking about?"

"This goes beyond you, Clint," Proctor said. "This is the murder of a policeman."

"What about Sally Rise?"

"The murder of a policeman is still the more

serious crime here," Proctor insisted.

"No, it isn't," Clint said. "Murder is murder."

"Sheriff Bush is working on her murder," Proctor said.

"And San Francisco is working on the murder of their policeman," Clint said.

"I've inherited that case."

"Remember," Clint said, "he's only wanted for questioning. You don't want to go in to the Bull's-eye and have to kill him . . . or do you?"

"No!" Proctor said. "What are you saying, that I *want* to kill Vic Ward?"

Clint shrugged.

"Maybe you've wanted to kill him for a long time," Clint said. "Maybe you've just been looking for a chance—a legal chance."

"No, no," Proctor said, shaking his head.

"You think that Ward has been keeping Loretta from marrying you, right?"

Proctor didn't answer.

"Tell me something, Sheriff," Clint said. "If I remember correctly, Loretta came here seven years ago, and Ward about four. Right?"

Still no answer.

"What about those first three years?" Clint asked. "Why didn't she marry you during those first three years?"

Proctor remained silent, staring at the top of the desk.

"Look, George," Clint said, "I'll help you get Ward, but let's get him alive, and let's get Loretta out at the same time."

"She'll never take the baby," Proctor said.

"Even if she doesn't," Clint said, "I want to help

her. Do you want to help her, or do you only want to help her if she'll marry you?"

Proctor lifted his eyes from the desk and stared at Clint.

"I want to help her."

"Then let's do it."

"How?"

"Well," Clint said, "now we're back to where we started. That's what we're here to figure out."

Vic Ward locked Loretta in his room and came storming down the hall. What he had in mind now was a glass of brandy, but Dan McGirt was blocking his path.

"Mr. Ward, what are you doing?"

"Get out of my way, McGirt."

McGirt stepped aside, and Ward entered his office. He went to his desk, poured a brandy, and drank it. McGirt entered the office and closed the door behind him.

"Mr. Ward—"

"I told you this is none of your business!"

"It *is* my business, sir." McGirt was trying to be respectful, while all he really wanted to do was strangle his employer. "We had men in the alley, sir, all ready to take care of Clint Adams when he tried to take Loretta out through her window. Now you've locked her in your room. Is there a window in your room?"

"No."

"Then we've missed our chance to take care of Clint Adams."

Ward thought furiously for a moment, then said, "No, we haven't."

"What do you mean?"

"Adams is supposed to come by and talk to Loretta again tonight."

"What are you proposing?"

"That we let him see her," Ward said.

"And then kill him?"

"That's right."

"In cold blood?" McGirt asked. "What's the sheriff gonna say?"

"Nothing," Ward said, "because it won't be in cold blood. He'll be killed trying to rape Loretta. You'll kill him protecting her."

McGirt thought a moment, then asked, "Will she go along with that?"

"She'll do whatever I tell her to do," Ward said, pouring another brandy.

"I hope you're right . . . sir."

"Don't worry," Ward said, "I'm right. Just get back to your post. I'll talk to you after I've spoken to her."

McGirt nodded and withdrew from the room. He hoped that Ward would be conscious long enough to set it up.

It actually wasn't that bad a plan.

In Ward's room Loretta tried the door and found it locked. She rattled the doorknob a few times before finally giving up. She looked around the room, but there was no other way in or out.

She walked over to Vic's dresser and looked in the mirror. Several strands of her hair had fallen free and were hanging down, giving her a disheveled look. She unpinned her hair, letting it all fall down to her shoulders.

What was she going to do now? Clint Adams's plan was ruined. Would he still come to see her tonight, as he was supposed to do? What if he didn't? What if he simply left in the morning with the baby, leaving Loretta right where she was when he got here, right where she had been for the past four years?

Actually, she had only been miserable the last three years she had been here in Doyle, and the first three. Those first three years she had still been smarting from what had happened to her in St. Louis. She had come out West to escape from the memory of that relationship, that life. She had even fought getting into a relationship with a decent man like George Proctor. Then Vic Ward came to town and bought the saloon where she worked. Immediately they had fallen into a relationship. She had loved Ward for over a year, and just when she was getting to the point where she thought she could be happy, Vic changed. He became the man she was still afraid of today. She was afraid to try to leave, and afraid to talk to George Proctor about it. Now, in spite of the fact that she offered him no encouragement, Clint Adams had come to town with Katherine, and was her only chance to get out, to get away from Vic Ward. Clint Adams was the only chance she had seen in three years, and might be the only chance she would ever see.

And now that chance was gone. Or was it?

Locked in and helpless, she was simply going to have to wait for others to decide her fate. Or was she?

She started going through Vic's drawers, and when she found what she wanted, she lifted her dress and tucked the object into the top of her stocking.

Now she sat down to wait and see what was going to happen.

THIRTY-FIVE

"It's getting dark," Proctor said. He was looking out the window of his office.

"That doesn't much matter, now," Clint said. "We would have needed the cover of darkness to get her out through her window. Now . . ."

Proctor ran his hands through his hair and returned to his desk. He picked up his empty coffee cup and scowled into it.

"Want some more coffee?" Proctor asked.

"Your coffee is terrible."

Proctor frowned.

"You've had four cups."

"It's taken me that long to work up the nerve to tell you the truth."

"Thanks," Proctor said. He made a face and put the cup back down on his desk. "Cigar?"

"You've had three already," Clint said, shaking his head. "It's a wonder you can still taste anything."

"You're just full of complaints," Proctor said, "aren't you?"

"That's what happens when you've been in a room together as long as we have." Clint stood up, placed his hands against the small of his back, and stretched.

"Look," Proctor said, "we're not coming up with anything this way. Let's consider the direct approach again."

"You mean the approach where a lot of people end up getting shot?"

"You know," Proctor said, "for someone with a reputation, you're unusually squeamish about using your gun."

"And you're not?"

"It's a tool of my trade," Proctor said. "I use it when I have to."

Clint walked to one of the walls of the office and put his hand against it.

"How thick are the walls of the saloon?"

Clint left the sheriff's office and went to check on the baby. Once again, Mrs. Gordon was taking care of Katherine.

"Katy is just fine, Clint," she said.

"Good, Mrs. Gordon."

"I think it's time you started calling me Sadie," Mrs. Gordon said.

"All right, Sadie," Clint said. "Uh, you might hear some commotion from the saloon tonight, Sadie. Stay away from the windows and the door when you do, all right?"

"What kind of commotion?"

"Oh, loud voices, noises . . . shooting."

"Oh," she said, "those kinds of noises."

"And stay with the baby."

"Is the baby in danger?"

"No," Clint said, but even after he said it, he wondered.

Vic Ward wouldn't send someone after an infant, would he?

Vic Ward was thinking about the baby. He left his office to go out and get McGirt. He spoke to McGirt right in the hall, without bothering to take him into his office.

"How much will you do for money?" he asked.

McGirt studied Ward for a few moments, then asked, "How much money?"

Ward smiled.

Clint hurried back to the sheriff's office.

"Do you have anyone in town who can use a gun?"

"You mean my deputies?" Proctor asked, shaking his head. "No, neither of them—"

"I mean anybody," Clint said. "Somebody I could hire."

"Hire?" Proctor asked. "To do what?"

Briefly, Clint explained.

"Ward wouldn't do that."

"You don't think so?" Clint asked. "The man's a heavy drinker, and I think he's starting to feel pretty desperate."

"But . . . over a woman?"

"How do you feel about Loretta?"

Proctor frowned and said, "Sure, I love her. I admit that, but I wouldn't go to *any* lengths—"

"We don't know what lengths we'll go to for a woman until we're tested," Clint said, "and I'm talking about all men."

"And you think Ward is at that point?"

"Yes."

"Let me think."

Clint walked to the door and opened it so some of the smoke in the room would drift out.

"We need someone who can shoot and someone who can be trusted."

"Right," Clint said, "and somebody with at least half a brain."

"Well, that leaves my deputies out right there."

"Well," Clint said, "come up with somebody."

"Wait a minute," Proctor said. "Last year a fella came to town and opened up a hardware store."

"So?"

"Let me finish," Proctor said. "The rumor around town when he got here was that he had just hung up his guns. I never heard of the fella, but that don't mean anything. I checked him out and he had no warrants. Since he's been here he's kept to himself, and I've never seen him wearing a gun. Maybe you know him."

"What's his name?"

"He calls himself Ken Kelly."

"Ken . . . Kelly? What's he look like?"

"Tall, black hair shot with gray, wide shoulders, big hands, black beard and mustache."

Clint had a thoughtful expression on his face.

"Know him?" Proctor asked.

"I might," Clint said. "Ever hear of a man named Kilkenny?"

"Kilkenny," Proctor said. "Now, that name rings a

bell. Jesus, you don't mean—Ken Kelly is Kilkenny? The gunman? Do you know him?"

"Well enough to know him when I see him."

"Well, let's go, then," Proctor said. "The hardware store is down two blocks, next to the barber. Kilken—I mean Ken Kelly—I mean, he lives in a room right behind it."

"No," Clint said, "I'll go. He might not react too well to your presence. In fact, I don't think you should even let him know that you know who he is."

"Why not?"

"If it is him, and he's changed his name, he's obviously trying to make a new life for himself," Clint explained. "What I'm doing is very unfair to him, but I can't be choosy, not tonight. Somebody's got to protect that baby."

"I see what you mean."

"My telling you who he is may finish him in this town if word gets around."

"You're asking me not to say anything."

"That's right."

"Well, if I remember right, Kilkenny's not wanted for anything."

"I wouldn't think so," Clint said. "He was handy with a gun, and had a rep, but he never was an outlaw."

"All right," Proctor said, "I don't see any reason to let it be known around town who he is. Do you think he'll help?"

"I don't know," Clint said. "I haven't seen him in about four years." He walked to the door and said, "All I can do is ask him."

THIRTY-SIX

Clint walked down to the hardware store and banged on the door until he saw a light inside. A face appeared at the window, taking him in, and he saw immediately that it *was* Kilkenny.

Kilkenny looked at him for a long time before opening the door. The man was shirtless, and the scars of his past life were very much in evidence on his body, which seemed to have no fat on it at all.

"Clint Adams," the man said.

"Hello, Tom."

"What's it been? Three years?"

"Four," Clint said. "Sante Fe."

"That's right," Kilkenny said. "Come on in."

Clint entered, and Kilkenny closed the door.

"In the back."

Clint followed Kilkenny into the back, where the light was. It was one room, with a bed, a dresser, and a chair, but not much more.

"Should I ask how you found me?"

"I wasn't looking for you, if that's what you mean," Clint said. "I'm here in town for a reason that has nothing to do with you."

"Then why are you here?"

"I need your help."

"I hung 'em up, Clint," Kilkenny said. "I'm in hardware now."

Clint stifled a joke about how each had been in hardware all his life.

"Let me explain the situation to you, Tom," Clint said, "and then you can tell me to go to hell."

"I can't tell you that now?" Kilkenny asked. "Oh, all right, go ahead and talk. I probably owe it to you to listen."

Clint explained to Kilkenny how he had come to be in Doyle and why he needed his help. It took a few minutes, and Kilkenny listened the whole time without commenting. When Clint was finished, he sat under Kilkenny's gaze for what seemed like several minutes before the man finally spoke.

"You sonofabitch."

"What?"

Kilkenny stood up and looked around for his shirt.

"A baby," he said, shaking his head and pulling on his shirt. "You managed to come up with the only thing I couldn't say no to, didn't you?"

"You'll help?"

"I won't strap on a gun, Clint," Kilkenny said, "but I'll grab a rifle and go over to the rooming house. I'll keep that baby safe for you."

"Thanks, Tom."

"Don't thank me," Kilkenny said. "There's a price."

"What price?"

Kilkenny pointed a finger at Clint and said, "When this is over, you're going to tell me how you knew I was here."

"Deal."

Clint walked Kilkenny to the rooming house and introduced him to Mrs. Gordon and Mrs. Muldoon. He used the name "Ken Kelly" in the introduction.

"You own the hardware store, don't you?" Mrs. Gordon asked.

"That's right."

"How did you get involved with this?"

"Just lucky." He looked at Clint and asked, "Who else is allowed in the house?"

"Me, the sheriff—do you know him?

"I've seen him."

"And a girl named Shannon. She works at the—"

"I know Shannon," Kilkenny said, a small smile touching his face.

"Uh-huh," Clint said. "That's it. Nobody else in."

"Deputies?"

"No."

"All right," Kilkenny said. "Mrs. Gordon, where will you and the baby be?"

"I have her in a room upstairs," Mrs. Gordon said. "I'm usually with her."

"Would it be possible to bring her down here, so we can all stay in the same room together?"

Mrs. Gordon looked at Clint, who said, "It sounds like a good idea to me."

"You told me the baby was in no danger," Mrs. Gordon said accusingly.

"This is just a precaution, Mrs. Gordon," he said. "You can do whatever Mr. Kelly says. He's very trustworthy."

"From you that's supposed to be comforting?" she said. She looked at Kilkenny and said, "I'll be right down with Katy."

"Mr. Kelly," Mrs. Muldoon said, "would you like some coffee?"

"Yes, thank you."

"Well," Clint said, "I can see you're all in good hands. I have to be going."

"Good luck," Kilkenny said. "You'll, uh, let me know when I can go home?"

"I appreciate this, Tom," Clint said, "I really do."

Kilkenny looked down at the rifle in his hand, as if it were a third arm that had suddenly sprouted, and said, "Yeah."

Clint walked back to the sheriff's office and found the man sitting at his desk, checking his gun.

"Well?" Proctor said.

"It's Kilkenny, all right," Clint said. "He's at the rooming house, watching the baby."

"How did you convince him?"

"I didn't," Clint said. "I just asked him."

"Just like that?" Proctor said, holstering his gun. "What's his price?"

"He, uh, wants me to tell him how I found him."

"You gonna tell him?"

Clint shrugged and said, "That's his price."

"Well," Proctor said, "I guess we'll deal with that tomorrow."

He stood up, walked to the window, and looked out. Then he looked at Clint over his shoulder.

"Are we going in?"

Clint nodded.

"Oh, yeah," he said, moving toward the door, "we're going in, all right."

THIRTY-SEVEN

Shannon headed for the curtained doorway and was stopped by McGirt, who stepped into her path.

"Where are you going?"

"The bartender needs a couple of bottles of bourbon," she said.

"Why can't he get them?"

"Because he's busy."

McGirt looked at the bar, where the bartender was busy pouring drinks.

"All right," McGirt said, "but make it fast."

He started to move out of her way, but as she took a step forward he stepped back into her way. The result was that she walked into him, her breasts bouncing off his chest.

"Ooh," he said.

"Very funny."

He moved aside, and she went down the hall. She looked behind her to see if he was watching her, but he wasn't. She stopped at Vic Ward's office door and touched the doorknob. She tried turning it, keeping as quiet as possible. She turned it just enough to determine that it wasn't locked, but not enough to alert him. That done, she moved on to the door to his room. When she tried that doorknob, she found that it wouldn't turn. It was locked. That was good enough for her.

She continued down the hall to get two bottles of bourbon.

When Clint entered the saloon he located McGirt first thing. The man in black was still occupying his corner. He spotted Clint and gave him an arrogant grin.

Clint walked to the bar and ordered a beer.

"Here's your beer," the bartender said, "and a little advice."

"Does the advice cost extra?" Clint asked.

"No."

"Go ahead."

"Get out of here."

"What kind of advice is that?"

"Good advice, friend," the bartender said. "I'm tellin' you for your own good."

"Thanks," Clint said. "I'll keep it in mind."

Clint worked on his beer and located Ward's other three men in the room. Or were they McGirt's men?

Shannon appeared at his elbow.

"Where is she?" Clint asked.

"Still back there," Shannon said. "The office door is unlocked, but the door to his room is locked."

"Get out of here and let Proctor know."

"Right."

"And then don't come back in."

"Clint—"

"I mean it, Shannon," he said tightly. "Don't come back."

She compressed her lips in annoyance, then said, "All right."

McGirt saw Shannon talking to Clint Adams. He caught the eye of his man nearest the door, and as Shannon started for it, the man blocked her way.

"Let me by, Gus," she said.

"Sorry."

She started to pass him, but he grabbed her by the wrist.

"Clint!" she called, because the man's grip was hurting her.

Clint turned and saw the man holding Shannon.

"Let her go!"

In the corner McGirt signaled to his other men to be ready.

"Adams!" he called.

Clint turned and saw McGirt moving toward him.

"Tell your man to let her go, McGirt."

"Why?" McGirt asked. "She works here. She's been taking too many breaks."

"Don't drag her into this, McGirt."

"Into what?" McGirt asked. "I didn't drag her into anything. I'm just doing my job. Shannon, go back to work, you hear?"

Shannon looked at Clint, who nodded.

Gus looked at McGirt, who also nodded. He released her wrist, and she moved away from him. The patrons of the saloon had stopped their drinking and gambling to see what was going on. They didn't understand it, but it all looked pretty interesting.

Clint watched McGirt, because the others wouldn't make a move without a signal from him.

Outside, down the street from the saloon, George Proctor was waiting for his signal. When it didn't come, he knew he was on his own. He moved to the alley and went through it, to the back of the saloon.

Farther down the street two of McGirt's men came out of another alley and started toward the other end of town, where the rooming house was located. Neither of them was very happy with the job he had been given to do, but they had been promised a lot of money to do it.

THIRTY-EIGHT

"I want to see Loretta Kane."

"Is that a fact?" McGirt said. "I guess we'll have to ask the boss about that, won't we?"

"Fine," Clint said, "let's ask him." He started to move away from the bar.

"Stand still, Adams," McGirt said. "My men know all about your big rep, and they're pretty nervous. You make a sudden move, and they might start shooting."

At the sound of the word "shooting" customers began to shift, moving toward some kind of cover. Pretty soon the center of the saloon was empty, as people pressed against the side walls. Some of them had even slipped out of the saloon behind Gus, who was still blocking the door.

"That would be their problem, wouldn't it?" Clint said.

McGirt's men were all armed with rifles as well as pistols. None of the rifles was pointed directly at Clint at the moment, but they were pointing in his general direction.

"So what are your orders, McGirt?" Clint asked. "Kill me?"

"That'd be up to you, wouldn't it?" McGirt asked.

"I'm sort of in a bind here," Clint said. "Even if I wanted to scratch my nose, that might trigger somebody's itchy finger, wouldn't it?"

McGirt smiled and said, "Then don't scratch."

Proctor managed to force open the back door of the saloon, and went inside. Clint had originally suggested that a stick of dynamite might blow out the wall in Ward's office, or his room, but then they had no way of knowing who would be directly on the other side of the wall. They wanted to get Loretta out, they didn't want to kill her.

Proctor found himself in a hallway, and at the far end he could see a curtained doorway. Since he had often seen that doorway from the other side, he knew where he was. He stood stock still and was able to hear voices. He could make out Clint's, and probably McGirt's. Apparently Clint had managed to get everyone's attention.

Proctor started down the hall, prepared to try every door until he found the right one.

Clint didn't move a muscle. He was facing four men with rifles, and he had no idea how proficient they were. If the time came for gun play, he was going to have to shoot to kill, and McGirt would have to be his first target. The others would take their cue from McGirt, and with him dead they might not react well.

"Well," Clint said to McGirt, "if you're going to earn your money, let's get to it."

"In good time."

"You sure you don't want to try me alone?" Clint asked. "Be a feather in your cap if you took me yourself, you know."

McGirt smiled and said, "Trying to goad me again, huh? What kind of moron do you take me for?"

"I don't know," Clint said. "How many kinds are there?"

Proctor found a locked door. Did he dare knock and check to see if she was in there? It might just be a locked storeroom.

Now, why lock a storeroom?

He braced his back against the wall opposite the door, then kicked out with his right foot. His heel struck the door just above the doorknob, and the door slammed open with the sound of a shot.

And then there *was* a shot!

At the sound of the shot, Clint drew his gun. McGirt's attention was diverted by the sound, and by the time he recovered, he was too late. As he tried to bring his rifle to bear on Clint, Clint fired. The bullet struck McGirt in the chest, knocking him backward.

Clint dropped into a crouch just as Gus fired. The bullet went over Clint's head and struck the mirror behind the bar. He fired, and Gus went staggering out through the batwing doors.

Clint rolled this time, across the floor as the other two men fired. . . .

• • •

Even at the other end of town, by the rooming house, the sounds of the shots could be heard.

"Mrs. Gordon," Kilkenny said, "take the baby and get down behind the sofa."

"Oh, my," Mrs. Gordon said.

Outside the rooming house the two men took the sounds of the shots as their cue. One went around back, and one approached the front. . . .

The shot went over Proctor's head as he entered the room. Loretta was standing there, holding a derringer in her hand. When she saw Proctor she gasped and dropped the gun, which she had taken from the top of her stocking.

"I thought it was Vic," she said, covering her mouth with her hands. "I could have killed you."

"At least," Proctor said. "Come on. . . ."

Clint came to a stop in a crouch, located a target, and fired. The man stumbled, coughed, and fell to the floor. But even as Clint turned to locate the fourth man, he knew he was going to be too late. The man was going to be able to get off at least one clear shot.

As he stared down the barrel of the man's rifle Clint heard a shot, and the man slammed back against the wall. Clint turned to see Proctor standing in the doorway, gun in hand. Next to him was Loretta Kane. He had his arm around her and looked like he was holding her up.

Clint stood up and waggled the barrel of his gun at Proctor.

Thanks.

• • •

Kilkenny figured two men, at least. That meant one front and one back. It had been a while, but it was all coming back to him.

They'd probably bust in as close together as possible. His edge was that he knew the inside of the house, and they didn't.

As the front door burst open, Kilkenny pointed his rifle and fired. The man had taken one step forward, and as the bullet struck him he took several quick steps back and fell off the porch.

Kilkenny turned and ran into the bedroom, where Mrs. Gordon and the baby were still behind the sofa, which he had pushed against the wall in anticipation of this moment. Mrs. Muldoon was behind one of the chairs, which had also been pressed to the wall.

Kilkenny stood ready, and as the other man came out of the kitchen, they fired at the same time.

Mrs. Gordon peeked up from behind the sofa and said, "Oh, my."

THIRTY-NINE

"Shannon!" Clint shouted.

"I'm here," she said, coming toward him.

"Are you all right?"

"I'm fine."

She came to him, and he hugged her with one arm. He still had his gun out. There was still Vic Ward to deal with.

The other people in the saloon began to file out, now that the lead had stopped flying.

Clint moved about the room checking bodies, making sure they were dead. Then he and Shannon approached Proctor and Loretta.

"Ward," Clint said.

"He must be in his office."

Clint and Proctor moved down the hall, with Shannon and Loretta behind them.

"That one," Loretta said, pointing to a door.

"You ready?" Clint asked Proctor.

"Yes."

"I'll go low, you go high," Clint said.

"Okay."

They both held their guns ready as Clint turned the doorknob and pushed the door open. They leaped into the room, low and high, their guns pointed in front of them. They both heard the snoring sound at the same time.

Draped over his desk was Victor Ward. There was an empty brandy bottle lying on its side next to his head, and he was snoring.

"Well," Proctor said, "he drank himself right out of the play, didn't he?"

"Maybe," Clint said, "but he also saved his own life by doing it."

Proctor turned to look at Loretta, who was staring at Ward.

"You're free of him now, Loretta," the lawman said. "He's under arrest, and he's going back to San Francisco."

"He's the devil," she said.

"If he is," Clint said, "he's now the devil without a kingdom to rule."

"Right," Proctor said. "God threw the devil out of heaven, and I'm throwing him out of town."

EPILOGUE

As it turned out, Ward was not going back to San Francisco immediately. First he was going to Tyler Falls, to stand trial for conspiracy to commit murder in the death of Sally Rise. Apparently he knew that Loretta's sister was on her way to Doyle. After Loretta's first letter from her sister saying she was coming, Ward hired a detective in St. Louis to keep an eye on her. As soon as she left St. Louis by train, he hired some men to make sure she never got there. They stopped the stage, dragged her off it, kept her and used her for a couple of days, and then killed her. This was learned from a man who was arrested by Sheriff Bush in Tyler Falls.

Ward also had to face charges in the attempted murder of Clint. When Proctor's deputy returned from Garnett with McGirt's man—his nose all bandaged—the man confessed that McGirt had paid him and the other man to kill Clint, and that McGirt had been paid in turn by Ward.

Somehow, somewhere, Vic Ward was going to end up in jail.

"Where's Loretta?" Clint asked Proctor.

"She's taken a room at the rooming house," Proctor said. "Mrs. Muldoon has never had so many rooms rented out at one time. Loretta's asleep."

"That's good."

"Are you leaving today?" Proctor asked.

"Now," Clint said. "My rig is outside." It had been three days since the shooting, and most of the loose ends had been tied up. No reason for him to stay around any longer.

"What about the baby?"

"That's up to Loretta," Clint said, "and maybe you. If she wants Katy, the baby is hers. If not, there's a man and woman back in Tyler Falls who'd just love to have her."

"I don't think so," Proctor said. "I think we can handle her. You gonna go say good-bye to her?"

"I said good-bye last night," Clint said. Truth of the matter was, it had been a very hard thing for him to do. If he went to see her again this morning, he might not want to leave.

Proctor put his hand out and said, "Thanks for all your help, Clint."

"And yours."

They shook hands.

"What about Kilkenny?" Clint asked. "I told him you knew who he was."

"We talked," Proctor said. "There's no reason for him to give up what he's started here. He's staying, and I'm keeping quiet."

"That's good."

"What about Shannon?"

Clint smiled. "I said good-bye to her last night, too. I'm all good-bye'd out, George. It's time for me to go."

Proctor walked Clint out and watched him climb onto the seat of his rig.

"Where you headed?"

"Someplace quiet," Clint said. "Someplace where there are no children."

He snapped the reins at his team and drove his rig out of town. He made sure he didn't pass the rooming house on his way out.

Watch for

KILLER'S GOLD

126th novel in the exciting GUNSMITH series
from Jove

Coming in June!

America's new star of the classic western

GILES TIPPETTE

author of *Hard Rock, Jailbreak* and *Crossfire,*
is back with his newest, most exciting novel yet

SIXKILLER

Springtime on the Half-Moon ranch has never been so hard. On top of running the biggest spread in Matagorda County, Justa Williams is about to become a daddy. Which means he's got a lot more to fight for when Sam Sixkiller comes to town. With his pack of wild cutthroats slicing a swath of mayhem all the way from Galveston, Sixkiller now has his ice-cold eyes on Blessing—and word has it he intends to pick the town clean.

Now, backed by men more skilled with branding irons than rifles, the Williams clan must fight to defend their dream—with their wits, their courage, and their guns. . . .

Turn the page
for a preview of
SIXKILLER
by Giles Tippette

Available now from Jove Books!

It was late afternoon when I got on my horse and rode the half mile from the house I'd built for Nora, my wife, up to the big ranch house my father and my two younger brothers still occupied. I had good news, the kind of news that does a body good, and I had taken the short run pretty fast. The two-year-old bay colt I'd been riding lately was kind of surprised when I hit him with the spurs, but he'd been lazing around the little horse trap behind my house and was grateful for the chance to stretch his legs and impress me with his speed. So we made it over the rolling plains of our ranch, the Half-Moon, in mighty good time.

I pulled up just at the front door of the big house, dropped the reins to the ground so that the colt would stand, and then made my way up on the big wooden porch, the rowels of my spurs making a *ching-ching* sound as I walked. I opened the big front door and let myself into the hall that led back to the main parts of the house.

I was Justa Williams and I was boss of all thirty-thousand deeded acres of the place. I had been so since it had come my duty on the weakening of our father, Howard, through two unfortunate incidents. The first had been the early demise of our mother, which had taken it out of Howard. That had been when he'd sort of started preparing me to take over the load. I'd been a hard sixteen or a soft seventeen at the time. The next level had jumped up when he'd got nicked in the lungs by a stray bullet. After that I'd had the job of boss. The place was run with my two younger brothers, Ben and Norris.

It had been a hard job but having Howard around had made the job easier. Now I had some good news for him and I meant him to take it so. So when I went clumping back toward his bedroom that was just off the office I went to yelling, "Howard! Howard!"

He'd been lying back on his daybed, and he got up at my approach and come out leaning on his cane. He said, "What the thunder!"

I said, "Old man, sit down."

I went over and poured us out a good three fingers of whiskey. I didn't even bother to water his as I was supposed to do because my news was so big. He looked on with a good deal of pleasure as I poured out the drink. He wasn't even supposed to drink whiskey, but he'd put up such a fuss that the doctor had finally given in and allowed him one well-watered whiskey a day. But Howard claimed he never could count very well and that sometimes he got mixed up and that one drink turned into four. But, hell, I couldn't blame him. Sitting around all day like he was forced to was enough to make anybody crave a drink even if it was just for something to do.

But now he seen he was going to get the straight stuff and he got a mighty big gleam in his eye. He took the glass when I handed it to him and said, "What's the occasion? Tryin' to kill me off?"

"Hell no," I said. "But a man can't make a proper toast with watered whiskey."

"That's a fact." he said. "Now what the thunder are we toasting?"

I clinked my glass with his. I said, "If all goes well you are going to be a grandfather."

"Lord A'mighty!" he said.

We said, "Luck" as was our custom and then knocked them back.

Then he set his glass down and said, "Well, I'll just be damned." He got a satisfied look on his face that I didn't reckon was all due to the whiskey. He said, "Been long enough in coming."

I said, "Hell, the way you keep me busy with this ranch's business I'm surprised I've had the time."

"Pshaw!" he said.

We stood there, kind of enjoying the moment, and then I nodded at the whiskey bottle and said, "You keep on sneaking drinks, you ain't likely to be around for the occasion."

He reared up and said, "Here now! When did I raise you to talk like that?"

I gave him a small smile and said, "Somewhere along the line." Then I set my glass down and said, "Howard, I've got to get to work. I just reckoned you'd want the news."

He said, "Guess it will be a boy?"

I give him a sarcastic look. I said, "Sure, Howard, and I've gone into the gypsy business."

Then I turned out of the house and went to looking for our foreman, Harley. It was early spring in the year of 1898 and we were coming into a swift calf crop after an unusually mild winter. We were about to have calves dropping all over the place, and with the quality of our crossbred beef, we couldn't afford to lose a one.

On the way across the ranch yard my youngest brother, Ben, came riding up. He was on a little prancing chestnut that wouldn't stay still while he was trying to talk to me. I knew he was schooling the little filly, but I said, a little impatiently, "Ben, either ride on off and talk to me later or make that damn horse stand. I can't catch but every other word."

Ben said, mildly, "Hell, don't get agitated. I just wanted to give you a piece of news you might be interested in."

I said, "All right, what is this piece of news?"

"One of the hands drifting the Shorthorn herd got sent back to the barn to pick up some stuff for Harley. He said he seen Lew Vara heading this way."

I was standing up near his horse. The animal had been worked pretty hard, and you could take the horse smell right up your nose off him. I said, "Well, okay. So the sheriff is coming. What you reckon we ought to do, get him a cake baked?"

He give me one of his sardonic looks. Ben and I were so much alike it was awful to contemplate. Only difference between us was that I was a good deal wiser and less hotheaded and he was an even size smaller than me. He said, "I reckon he'd rather have whiskey."

I said, "I got some news for you but I ain't going to tell you now."

"What is it?"

I wasn't about to tell him he might be an uncle under such circumstances. I gave his horse a whack on the rump and said, as he went off, "Tell you this evening after work. Now get, and tell Ray Hays I want to see him later on."

He rode off, and I walked back to the ranch house thinking about Lew Vara. Lew, outside of my family, was about the best friend I'd ever had. We'd started off, however, in a kind of peculiar way to make friends. Some eight or nine years past Lew and I had had about the worst fistfight I'd ever been in. It occurred at Crook's Saloon and Cafe in Blessing, the closest town to our ranch, about seven miles away, of which we owned a good part. The fight took nearly a half an hour, and we both did our dead level best to beat the other to death. I won the fight, but unfairly. Lew had had me down on the saloon floor and was in the process of finishing me off when my groping hand found a beer mug. I smashed him over the head with it in a last-ditch effort to keep my own head on my shoulders. It sent Lew to the infirmary for quite a long stay; I'd fractured his skull. When he was partially recovered Lew sent word to me that as soon as he was able, he was coming to kill me.

But it never happened. When he was free from medical care Lew took off for the Oklahoma Territory, and I didn't hear another word from him for four years. Next time I saw him he came into that very same saloon. I was sitting at a back table when I saw him come through the door. I eased my right leg forward so as to clear my revolver for a quick draw from the holster. But Lew just came up, stuck out his hand in a friendly gesture, and said he wanted to let bygones be bygones. He offered to buy me a drink, but I had a bottle on the table so I just told him to get himself a glass and take advantage of my hospitality.

Which he did.

After that Lew became a friend of the family and was important in helping the Williams family in about three confrontations where his gun and his savvy did a good deal to turn the tide in our favor. After that we ran him against the incumbent sheriff who we'd come to dislike and no longer trust. Lew had been reluctant at first, but I'd told him that money couldn't buy poverty but it could damn well buy the sheriff's job in Matagorda County. As a result he got elected, and so far as I was concerned, he did an outstanding job of keeping the peace in his territory.

Which wasn't saying a great deal because most of the trouble he had to deal with, outside of helping us, was the occasional Saturday night drunk and the odd Main Street dogfight.

So I walked back to the main ranch house wondering what he wanted. But I also knew that if it was in my power to give, Lew could have it.

I was standing on the porch about five minutes later when he came riding up. I said, "You want to come inside or talk outside?"

He swung off his horse. He said, "Let's get inside."

"You want coffee?"

"I could stand it."

"This going to be serious?"

"Is to me."

"All right."

I led him through the house to the dining room, where we generally, as a family, sat around and talked things out. I said, looking at Lew, "Get started on it."

He wouldn't face me. "Wait until the coffee comes. We can talk then."

About then Buttercup came staggering in with a couple of cups of coffee. It didn't much make any difference about what time of day or night it was, Buttercup might or might not be staggering. He was an old hand of our father's who'd helped to develop the Half-Moon. In his day he'd been about the best horse breaker around, but time and tumbles had taken their toll. But Howard wasn't a man to forget past loyalties so he'd kept Buttercup on as a cook. His real name was Butterfield, but me and my brothers had called him Buttercup, a name he clearly despised, for as long as I could remember. He was easily the best shot with a long-range rifle I'd ever seen. He had an old .50-caliber Sharps buffalo rifle, and even with his old eyes and seemingly unsteady hands he was deadly anywhere up to five hundred yards. On more than one occasion I'd had the benefit of that seemingly ageless ability. Now he set the coffee down for us and give all the indications of making himself at home. I said, "Buttercup, go on back out in the kitchen. This is a private conversation."

I sat. I picked up my coffee cup and blew on it

and then took a sip. I said, "Let me have it, Lew."

He looked plain miserable. He said, "Justa, you and your family have done me a world of good. So has the town and the county. I used to be the trash of the alley and y'all helped bring me back from nothing." He looked away. He said, "That's why this is so damn hard."

"What's so damned hard?"

But instead of answering straight out he said, "They is going to be people that don't understand. That's why I want you to have the straight of it."

I said, with a little heat, "Goddammit, Lew, if you don't tell me what's going on I'm going to stretch you out over that kitchen stove in yonder."

He'd been looking away, but now he brought his gaze back to me and said, "I've got to resign, Justa. As sheriff. And not only that, I got to quit this part of the country."

Thoughts of his past life in the Oklahoma Territory flashed through my mind, when he'd been thought an outlaw and later proved innocent. I thought maybe that old business had come up again and he was going to have to flee for his life and his freedom. I said as much.

He give me a look and then made a short bark that I reckoned he took for a laugh. He said, "Naw, you got it about as backwards as can be. It's got to do with my days in the Oklahoma Territory all right, but it ain't the law. Pretty much the opposite of it. It's the outlaw part that's coming to plague me."

It took some doing, but I finally got the whole story out of him. It seemed that the old gang he'd fallen in with in Oklahoma had got wind of his being the sheriff of Matagorda County. They thought that Lew was still the same young hellion and that they had them a bird nest on the ground, what with him being sheriff and all. They'd sent word that they'd be in town in a few days and they figured to "pick the place clean." And they expected Lew's help.

"How'd you get word?"

Lew said, "Right now they are raising hell in Galveston, but they sent the first robin of spring down to let me know to get the welcome mat rolled out. Some kid about eighteen or nineteen. Thinks he's tough."

"Where's he?"

Lew jerked his head in the general direction of Blessing. "I throwed him in jail."

I said, "You got me confused. How is you quitting going to help the situation? Looks like with no law it would be even worse."

He said, "If I ain't here maybe they won't come. I plan to send the robin back with the message I ain't the sheriff and ain't even in the country. Besides, there's plenty of good men in the county for the job that won't attract the riffraff I seem to have done." He looked down at his coffee as if he was ashamed.

I didn't know what to say for a minute. This didn't sound like the Lew Vara I knew. I understood he wasn't afraid and I understood he thought he was doing what he thought was the best for everyone concerned, but I didn't think he was thinking too straight. I said, "Lew, how many of them is there?"

He said, tiredly, "About eighteen all told. Counting the robin in the jail. But they be a bunch of rough hombres. This town ain't equipped to handle such. Not without a whole lot of folks gettin' hurt. And I won't have that. I figured on an argument from you, Justa, but I ain't going to make no battlefield out of this town. I know this bunch. Or kinds like them." Then he raised his head and give me a hard look. "So I don't want no argument out of you. I come out to tell you what was what because I care about what you might think of me. Don't make me no mind about nobody else but I wanted you to know."

I got up. I said, "Finish your coffee. I got to ride over to my house. I'll be back inside of half an hour. Then we'll go into town and look into this matter."

He said, "Dammit, Justa, I done told you I—"

"Yeah, I know what you told me. I also know it ain't really what you want to do. Now we ain't going to argue and I ain't going to try to tell you what to do, but I am going to ask you to let us look into the situation a little before you light a shuck and go tearing out of here. Now will you wait until I ride over to the house and tell Nora I'm going into town?"

He looked uncomfortable, but, after a moment, he nodded. "All right," he said. "But it ain't going to change my mind none."

I said, "Just go in and visit with Howard until I get back. He don't get much company and even as sorry as you are you're better than nothing."

That at least did make him smile a bit. He sipped at his coffee, and I took out the back door to where my horse was waiting.

Nora met me at the front door when I came into the house. She said, "Well, how did the soon-to-be grandpa take it?"

I said, "Howard? Like to have knocked the heels off his boots. I give him a straight shot of whiskey in celebration. He's so damned tickled I don't reckon he's settled down yet."

"What about the others?"

I said, kind of cautiously, "Well, wasn't nobody else around. Ben's out with the herd and Norris is in Blessing. Naturally Buttercup is drunk."

Meanwhile I was kind of edging my way back toward our bedroom. She followed me. I was at the point of strapping on my gunbelt when she came into the room. She said, "Why are you putting on that gun?"

It was my sidegun, a .42/40-caliber Colts revolver that I'd been carrying for several years. I had two of them, one that I wore and one that I carried in my saddlebags. The gun was a .40-caliber chambered weapon on a .42-caliber frame. The heavier frame gave it a nice feel in the hand with very little barrel deflection, and the .40-caliber slug was big enough to stop any thing you could hit solid. It had been good luck for me and the best proof of that was that I was alive.

I said, kind of looking away from her, "Well, I've got to go into town."

"Why do you need your gun to go into town?"

I said, "Hell, Nora, I never go into town without a gun. You know that."

"What are you going into town for?"

I said, "Norris has got some papers for me to sign."

"I thought Norris was already in town. What does he need you to sign anything for?"

I kind of blew up. I said, "Dammit, Nora, what is with all these questions? I've got business. Ain't that good enough for you?"

She give me a cool look. "Yes," she said. "I don't mess in your business. It's only when you try and lie to me. Justa, you are the worst liar in the world."

"All right," I said. "All right. Lew Vara has got some trouble. Nothing serious. I'm going to give him a hand. God knows he's helped us out enough." I could hear her maid, Juanita, banging around in the kitchen. I said, "Look, why don't you get Juanita to hitch up the buggy and you and her go up to the big house and fix us a supper. I'll be back before dark and we'll all eat together and celebrate. What about that?"

She looked at me for a long moment. I could see her thinking about all the possibilities. Finally she said, "Are you going to run a risk on the day I've told you you're going to be a father?"

"Hell no!" I said. "What do you think? I'm going in to use a little influence for Lew's sake. I ain't going to be running any risks."

She made a little motion with her hand. "Then why the gun?"

"Hell, Nora, I don't even ride out into the pasture without a gun. Will you quit plaguing me?"

It took a second, but then her smooth, young face calmed down. She said, "I'm sorry, honey. Go and help Lew if you can. Juanita and I will go up to the big house and I'll personally see to supper. You better be back."

I give her a good, loving kiss and then made my adieus, left the house, and mounted my horse and rode off.

But I rode off with a little guilt nagging at me. I swear, it is hell on a man to answer all the tugs he gets on his sleeve. He gets pulled first one way and then the other. A man damn near needs to be made out of India rubber to handle all of them. No, I wasn't riding into no danger that March day, but if we didn't do something about it, it wouldn't be long before I would be.